Gerald Massey

A tale of eternity and other poems

Gerald Massey

A tale of eternity and other poems

ISBN/EAN: 9783337174330

Printed in Europe, USA, Canada, Australia, Japan

Cover: Foto ©Andreas Hilbeck / pixelio.de

More available books at **www.hansebooks.com**

A TALE OF ETERNITY

And other Poems

And other Poems

By GERALD MASSEY

Audere Spei

STRAHAN & CO., PUBLISHERS

56 LUDGATE HILL, LONDON

1870

VIRTUE AND CO., PRINTERS, CITY ROAD, LONDON.

CONTENTS.

A RHYME FOR THE READER.

A SINGER sang in sleep, and, sleeping, dream'd
  He sang divinely, while his spirit seem'd
So far in Music's heaven to soar and sing,
They could not follow who stood listening !
For him, the soul of sweetness found a voice.
For them, the Singer only " made a noise."

Such is the difference in the uttered strain,
From that fine music passing thro' the brain.
Such sumless treasures we possess in dreams,
To find at waking only mirrored gleams.
No revelation of the written word
Will render all the spirit saw and heard.

So fresh they breathed ; so faded now they look
My few poor withered flowers shut in a book.
Gone is the glory that once gleamed from them ;
The Spirit of Light imprisoned in the gem
Now the wing'd life hath settled down in words,
These are but stuffed instead of Singing Birds.

Feelings brimful of warmth as is a rose
Of its June-red, have lost their perfumed glows ;
The heaven-revealing thoughts that star-like shone,
The daily kindlings of eternal dawn,—
All darkened down, like Meteors that have birth
In Heaven, to flash and quench them cold in
     earth.

We grasp at diamonds visible in the dew,
And open empty tear-wet hands to you !
We clasp at heart the daughters of the skies,
Their shadow stays with us ; the substance flies.
Glimpses divine will peep ; pictures will pass,
And leave no likeness on the Seer's glass.

The Poet's best, immortally will lurk
In that rare motion of his soul at work.

Bee-like, he brings you one gold honey-drop ;
But, the full-swing, high on the flower-top,
'Twixt Heaven that rained itself in sweetness down,
And Earth—all bloom for him—is ne'er made
known.

MY poem was in the making.   These are your
Warmth-needy nurslings, Reader ! mine no more.
The life I gave will no more fill my breast
Than the flown birds come back to last year's nest.
And if these live again, 'tis you must give
The reflex thrill to them by which they live.

You must make out the music from the hint
Prelusive : I but tune the instrument.
The glory or the gladness or the grace
Must shine for me re-orient in your face.
The seed, that in my life took secret root,
In yours must bud, and flower, and bear the fruit.

A TALE OF ETERNITY.

B

"*Among the rest, a small unsightly root,*
But of divine effect, he culled me out ;
The leaf was darkish, and had prickles on it,
But in another country, as he said,
Bore a bright golden flower."—MILTON.

"*Now a thing was secretly brought to me, and mine ear received a*
little thereof : in visions of the night, when deep sleep falleth on men,
fear came upon me, and trembling ; then a spirit passed before my face
and the hair of my flesh stood up : an image was before mine eyes ;
there was silence, and I heard a voice."—BOOK OF JOB.

"*He maketh His angels spirits ; His ministers a flaming fire.*"
PSALMS OF DAVID.

"*Millions of spiritual creatures walk the earth*
Unseen, both when we wake and when we sleep."
MILTON.

"*I've seen some men, veracious, nowise mad,*
Who have thought or dreamed, declared and testified
They heard the Dead a-ticking like a clock
Which strikes the hours of the eternities,
Beside them, with their natural ears,—and known
That human spirits feel the human way
And hate the unreasoning awe which waves them off
From possible communion. It may be."—MRS. BROWNING.

A TALE OF ETERNITY.

AS One who, in a strange and far Country,
    In presence of his future Bride may be,
That keeps the secret of her face concealed,
Until, as Wife, the Maiden stands revealed :
And who doth make blind guesses at the face ;
Its wealth of nature and its gifts of grace :
Much marvelling if the form beneath the folds
Be like the picture that at heart he holds :
And who, as chance befall, doth furtively
Feel the hid features that he may not see—
Trying to gather, at a Lover's touch,
The least of all he longs to know so much :
Even thus, before the Next World's face I stand,
And o'er its clouded features pass my hand ;
Groping to get where mortal sight doth fail,
Some inkling of the face behind the Veil !

It is the voice of Vision in the night:
I learned in darkness what I speak in light.
Perchance such ne'er attains the perfect True
And yet may utter meaning for the few,
As sandiest desert wastes reflect afar
Light from our Sun to some benighted Star!

PART I

NIGHT after night I wakened with a start;
        The coldness of a gravestone at my heart;
As tho' I had been nearly caught by Death
Who imaged Sleep to kiss away my breath!
The silence lookt so ominous, the gloom
Just losing shape and feature in the room.
Had I but wakened sooner, without doubt,
I should have found some dreadful secret out.
Nothing to grapple with; nothing to see;
Yet something fearful there must somewhere be;
Grim shadows grew from out their hiding-nook;
A strange life lurked in the familiar look
Of innocent things, as tho' upon the eve
Of issuing, terrible as its prey perceive
The *Mantis* in the likeness of a leaf,
Changed in a moment to a Murderous Thief.
I peered out of the window, nothing there
But the vast heavens with all their loneness bare—

The phantom presence of Immensity
That from behind its dumb mask whispered me.

At times a noise, as tho' a dungeon door
Had grated, with set teeth, against the floor :
A ring of iron on the stones ; a sound
As if of granite into powder ground ;
A pickaxe and a spade at work ! sad sighs
As of a wave that sobs and faints and dies.
And then a shudder of the house ; a scrawl
As tho' a knife scored letters in the wall.
About the room a gush and gurgle went,
As if the water-pipe got sudden vent ;
Drop after drop, I heard it plop, and ping,
Into some vessel, with metallic ring.
Yet, on these very nights there was no rain !
And then, betwixt the ear's suspense and strain,
A faint voice crying in the air or brain.

The wind would rise and wail most humanly
With a low scream of stifled agony
Over the birth of life about to be.
Thro' all the house its coldest wave hath rusht,
Altho' a moment since the night was husht.

And ere the hurried gust had ceased to moan,
The dreaming dog would answer with a groan.
On nights of wind and rain the sounds were worst;
More live the portent the black midnight hearst.

At times I seemed to waken at a call
And rose up listening for the next footfall
Which never came, as tho' it could not keep
The step with that my spirit caught in sleep,
For I, in waking, must have crossed the line
Bounding the range of spirit-life from mine.
I felt the Presence on that other side
Grope where some secret door might open wide.
I knew the brain might strike the electric spark
Which should make live this phantom of the Dark.
Once as I woke I could have sworn I saw
A white face from the window-pane withdraw!
But, softly in its place the curtain slid,
Even in the uplifting of the swift eyelid.

Sometimes I woke with lashes wet and bright
With a strange glory of delicious light,
As tho' an Angel had shone my shut eyes thro'
And filled my soul with heaven, as Dawn the dew:

A fragrance from afar with me would stay
And at my work my heart sang all next day.

I am no Coward; never could believe
That spirits do their hell or heaven leave
To walk by night in the old human ways.
For forty years this was my creed o' days.
Somehow the dark another tale doth tell:
We are so fearful of the Unfathomable!
The Infinite is full of whisperings;
With mortal tug the wildered spirit clings
To its known shore of firm reality,
Yet feels drawn outward—like the ebbing sea
That hugs its beach so closely and in vain—
In this vast ebb of Being to its main.

And it is eerie in the night to lie
Lonesome, all naked to the awful sky—
This secret spawning-time of hell on earth
When mist and midnight give the toadstools birth,
And worlds of shy leaf-shadowed life steal forth,—
What time the Powers of Darkness have their
      day;
Our world asleep and Heaven so far away:

When in the shroud-like stillness there may be
Shapes moving round us that we do not see !

Our little sphere of life is darkly rimmed
In the wide universe of Being brimmed
With life perhaps inimical to us !
Nor could we live if all were luminous.
But is it certain we have lost the sight
They had of old in watches of the night,
Who heard the voices, saw the shape that stood
Before them in God's own similitude ?
They saw with eyes of spirit—Heaven keep
The veil of flesh about me dark and deep !

What does the Darkness mutter?   Is it Death
That makes the light burn bluer with his breath ?
Was that a creaking of the stair? a Rat
Nibbling the wainscot? did a flittering Bat
Flap at the window?   Floors will crack for sure,
But may not unseen feet be on the floor?
Spirits stand rapping at Life's outer gate,
And, if we dare not open, will they wait?
Was that the Death-Watch ticking in the wall?
One's hair—alive—begins to coldly crawl.

Is there some Whispering Gallery of the ear,
In which the other world we overhear?
The very Mirror is a doorway, thro'
Whose dark another face may look at you!
It haunts you, gliding as the Moonbeams glide,
Like waters wan that counsel suicide.

Who knows with what those ghostly gleams are
    rife
In spectral semblance of our sunlit life?
What Night hath shielded from pursuing Day
In sanctuary darkness, hid away,
As Paramour of hers in some foul play?
What viewless horrors in the wind may lurk,
That fill the mind with Shadows eerie and murk;
Perhaps the Devil audibly at work?
Maybe the voices of a sunless world
That in the eclipse of night is doomward hurled
What groping outcasts of ignoble soul
Are working thro' the darkness, like the mole,
Crouching in dreams to steal on sleeping Men.
Red-handed spirits that flung life back again
To Him who gave, and hide their murder-mark
In any secret corner of the dark:

What phantom shapes forlorn may meet and march
In long procession under Night's dark arch,
Stretching their arms to us, worm-fretted, all
Hueless and featureless and weirdly tall :
What rootless strays of life are ever blown
About like floating ghosts of thistle-down
That seek a foothold and are whirled away :
Dead leaves a-dancing—vanishing sea-spray ;
Night-wandering souls, without a house or shore,
That roam life's border-world for evermore
Homeless, as drifted clouds are driven past
Their heaven for ever, by the hurrying blast.

And now we come to think, may we not hold
Ghost-hands in ours, that turn them icy cold ?
A ghostly presence whitens in the cheek
And makes the blood run water,—wan and
    weak
The swooning life from out us faintly fleets,
And turns to drops at the chill touch it meets.
The walls of flesh are waxing all too thin
To keep the world of spirits from crowding in.
We wrap the clothes about us ; but, still bare
In soul, we feel a wave of chillier air,

Like that which brings the dawn, but that's a breath
Of sweet new life, this hath an odour of death !
The spirit spiracles all open wide
And life seems drowning in the flooding tide ;
We cannot cry, the Unseen world doth strive
To seal the mouth and bury the soul alive.
I must believe in Ghosts, lying awake
With them o' nights, when flesh will pimple and quake,
And lustily one pulls the Bell of Prayer,
From this thick snow of spirits to clear the air.

No marvel that the Birds salute the Dawn,
For all the dangers of the dark withdrawn ;
Break into singing with their first free breath,
That they have swum the dim, vast sea of death,
And hymn the resurrection of the Light,
In praise to Him who kept them thro' the night
And cared for his least little feathered things,
Encompassed with the safety of His Wings ;
While those, that cannot warble, twittering tell
Of darkness passed once more and all is well.

With what a thankful heart I've often heard
The blessed cry of Morning's earliest Bird !

How eagerly watcht the weird and waning Night
Turn deathly pale and pass away in light.
Yet, I believe that God is master still.
He reigneth; He whose lightest breath could thrill
The universe of worlds like drops of dew,
And if the Spirit-world hath broken thro'
It cannot be unknown, unseen by Him;
It must be with His will, not their mere whim.
And if our world of breath be set aflood,
Swimming in supernatural neighbourhood,
There is a soul within will not be drowned,
Even tho' a sea of spirits surges round:
An inner infinite with power to reach
The level of its outer ocean-beach!
Therefore I trust Him; shut mine eyes and say
" *Lead on, O Lord, Thou only know'st the way!*
Father in Heaven, take my hand in Thine;
Be at my heart, and in my countenance shine.
Then, all unfearing, shall I face the gate
At which the powers of Darkness lie in wait."

PART II

ONCE on a time, the ancient story saith,
    Some foolish Mummers danced a masque of
        Death.
They bore his emblems, trying, every one,
To out-parody the bony Skeleton ;
And, as the merriment grew, there glided in
Grim Death Himself, mocking with ghastly grin
At their poor make-believe ; as who should say
" *This is the real thing and no mere play.*"

" Talk of the Devil," say we, "and he's here,"
Sudden as thunder-claps, when skies are clear.

'Twas thus all fears and phantoms of the past,
Shaped into something palpable at last.

One night, as I lay musing on my bed,
The veil was rent that shows the Dead not dead.

Upon a Picture I had fixed mine eyes,
Till slowly it began to magnetise.
So the Ecstatics on their symbol stare,
Until the Cross fades and the Christ is there !
Thus, while I mused upon the picture's face,
A veil of white mist wavered in its place ;
And to a lulling motion I sank deep,
With spirit awake and senses all asleep,
Down thro' an air that palpitatingly
Breathed with a breath of life unknown to me ;
And when the motion ceased, against the
    gloom,
There lived another Form within the room,
Suddenly, strange and horrible, as rise
The Torturers that stare in dying eyes :
Or, as the Serpent—ere a leaf be stirred—
Looks thro' the dark on some bewildered bird :
A face in which the life had burned away
To cinders of the soul and ashes grey :
The forehead furrowed with a sombre frown
That seemed the image, in shadow, of Death's
    crown ;
His look a map of misery that told
How all the under-world in blackness rolled.

A human face in hideous eclipse;
No lustre in the hair, no life on lips;
The faintest gleam of corpse-light, lurid, wan,
Showed me the lying likeness of a Man!
The old soiled lining of some mortal dress:
A Spirit sorely stained with earthiness.

But, almost ere I could have time to fear,
I saw what seemed an Angel standing near,
With face like His who wore the old thorn
        crown;
In whose dear person very Love came down.
And on his face a smile for my relief:
A dream of glory in my night of grief,
Shedding an influent mildness thro' the awe,
Pleasant to feel, as was the smile I saw:
Indeed, methought he breathed a fragrance faint,
That overcame some rotting tomby taint.
He wore a purple vesture thin as mist,
The Breath of Dawn, upon the plum dew-kissed.
No flame-hued, flame-shaped, Golden-Holly tree
Ere kindled at the sun so splendidly
As that self-radiant head, with lifted hair
A-wave in many a fiery scimitar.

We think of Shades as native to the night;
We photograph the other world in white,
That will not paint its tints upon our sight.
But there are Colours of the Eternal Light,
And this was of them; pulsing such live
    glows
As never reddened blood or ripened rose:
No Mist from the past life as we have deemed
The Dead to be; no pallid shadow dreamed
By Greeks of old, but Life itself this seemed.
And such a light was in the Angel's face,
It made a glory round about the place
To see by: as you mark in the gold ray
The Motes that dance invisibly in the grey.
But, deep in shadow of his inner night,
The Dark Shape stood and sinned against the
    Light.

As men have felt, when earth rockt underfoot,
Their trust in it was wrencht up by the root;
The firm foundations of all things had given,
And any instant they might be in heaven:
As one midway across a wide, white road,
In winter, when all night the skies have snowed,

Learns 'tis not earth but frozen stream beneath,
And he is leaning on the arms of Death:
So did I feel to find our earthy bound
Of Substance was no longer safe or sound;
That spirit-springs make quicksand of firm ground;
That spirit-hands withdraw our curtains round;
That spirit between particles can pass
Surely and visibly, as light thro' glass;
With power to come and go, stand upright, loom
Dense to the eye, outlined against the gloom.

The Dark Shape on me turned its eyes of guile,
Sullen yet fierce.   I read the wicked smile
That sneered—"*Behold the cause of all your fear!*
You need not shudder tho' while He is near."
And then he spoke, or seemed to speak, in words,
Altho' I saw his thoughts like murderous swords,
Or toothëd wheels, go whirling round within
The fearsome face so shadowy and thin,
And did not always need the speech to know
What dreadful thing it was he had to show.

"*Lo! I am one of those doomed souls who dwell*
In Heaven's vast Shadow which the Good call Hell.

Lo ! I am he, the gloomy sneak, who did
The deed of darkness, fancying all was hid :
The Awful eyes being on me all the while,
And Devils pointing at me with their smile.
I carry such a hell within my breast,
That all about me throbs with my unrest,
As tho' the heavens were shaken, or the earth
Were overtaken in the throes of birth ;
Doors tremble open, walls disintegrate,
And thro' the sense the soul keeps open gate !
With such a pulse of power my pangs awake
At midnight, that from sleep they sometimes shake
You ! Matter, with Mind's thrillings, doth so
    quake,
That atoms from their fellow atoms start,
As tho' they felt the heave of some live heart."

Then seeing the questioning wonder in my look,
He answered, as my turn of thought he took,

" Yes, it is true, all true, the thing you dreamed ;
Most real is the life that only seemed.
Soul's no mere shadow that gross substance throws ;
Our passions are not pageantary shows,

Exhaled from Matter, like the cloud from cape,
They are the life's own lasting final shape.
This scheme of things with all the sights you see,
Are only pictures of the things that be.
What you call Matter is but as the sheath,
Shaped, even as bubbles are, by spirit-breath.
The mountains are but firmer clouds of earth,
Still changing to the breath that gave them birth.
Spirit aye shapeth Matter into view,
As Music wears the forms it passes thro'.
Spirit is lord of substance, Matter's sole
First cause and forming power and final goal."

And who is this, I asked, that in his face
Doth image humanly celestial grace;
That calms my soul as when the Moon looks forth,
Whose smile in heaven makes stillness on the
          earth?

" One of those Ministers who are sent below
To walk the earth, patrolling to and fro,
As sentinels on guard, night after night,
That in the darkness make a watch-fire light,

Lest sleeping souls be helplessly surprised
By mad wild beasts of worlds not realised."

I lookt, the shining face serenely smiled
Away all terror like a thing beguiled.

" One of the dreadful Angels of the Lord,
Who are his fiery-flaming two-edged sword,
Which at each door and window waves and burns
Until the Angel of the Dawn returns.,
They are with you, watching thro' the murkest hour,
And seen, or unseen, hold us in their power,
That when the devil rages in us, lo !
We strike and strike and yet there falls no blow.
They mesmerise us standing there behind,
And, as in dreams, we struggle bound and blind.
The sharpest tortures that I have to bear
Are when I feel his presence hovering near.
A ray from heaven turns to a sword in hell;
The flash is maddening, we so darkly dwell !
The heat of heaven is like the blazing ring
Of fire that makes the Scorpion try to sting
Itself to death ; an air of Heaven's breath
Is poison ; hell is spiritual death :

And this awakes us, with its stir and strife,
Like tinglings of the drowned recalled to life."

I glanced again : I saw the look arise
As of a drawn Sword in the Angel's eyes.

" *We have met here for years.   He comes to see*
Me digging nightly; grope for my lost key;
Gives me his countenance, and but for him
I might work hidden in the shadows dim.
His presence kindles round me such a light,
All heaven can see me prowling thro' the night;
All hell make merry at the gruesome sight.

" *I never told my secret in your world,*
I kept it at the heart too closely curled;
There, at my lifesprings, did I nestle and nurse
The hidden snake, my bosom's clinging curse;
My worm of torment biting bitterly,
And fed it fat for all eternity.
And no eye saw it writhe in my white face,
Or heard it hiss in its dark hiding-place,
When any voice of secret murders told,
And in its might it wantoned and grew bold.

It gnawed my heart as with hell-fire for years.
Drink would not drown it, nor a sea of tears
Quench it, nor all the waters of the land
Whiten my soul, or wash my red right hand !
Whate'er I did, my heart with hell-fire burned;
Mine eyes with redness swam where'er I turned.
I dared not slumber soundly, lest asleep
The unsleeping secret from my lips should leap
In dreams, and I on waking might have found
Myself had turned Informer, and was bound
In handcuffs, with the accusing faces round.

" And so, at last, I pricked the bubble of breath,
I plunged to hide me from Myself in death :
I found the hell-hole in the wild whirlpool ;
Plucked the cold hand down on my brain to cool :
I grovelled out my own deep grave ; I fell
Right thro' it, into open arms of hell.

" I fancied, when I took the headlong leap,
That death must be an everlasting sleep ;
And the white Winding-sheet and green sod might
Shut out the world, and I have done with sight.

Cold water from my hand had washt the warm
And crimson carnage ; safe the little form
Lay underground : the tiny trembling waif
Of life hid from the light; my secret safe.
In vain.   You cannot hide a deed like this,
With all the heavens a cloud of witnesses :
Useless to blot the blood out with the dust,
When it hath eaten with its ruddy rust
Into your spirit's hand, where, visibly
The murder-stain leers thro' eternity !
Look there."

    I lookt and saw what seemed a hand
Of blood-stained shadow, kindling like a brand
When breathed on ! it so brightened as he sighed;
Plucking it from his breast where he did hide
Its guilty red.

     " *That hand once gripped the knife*
That slew my child.   This is its ruddy life,
Red-hot; on fire of hell !   In burning rings,
The blood my fingers clutcht, for ever clings,
And clamps them with relentless ache and smart
So closely that they will not pull apart.
Once only, while I wept and almost prayed,
They yielded just a little : then was played

A trick of Demons on me; all between,
They shone, thin-webbed with gore, and clearly seen
As thro' a window, thro' the web, there smiled
Up in my face the face of my dead child.
Better to bear this fiery grip of pain,
Than they should open on that sight again.

" The whirling world had flung my life from it.
And I felt falling thro' the Infinite,
For weeks and months, and years on years of nights
Innumerable, from stupendous heights ;
For, as a minute's slumber may be all
As one with that of a million years, my fall
So quickened being, that a minute's fears
Made instantaneous a million years.
No God to call upon, no power to stay,
No hand to clutch at on my endless way !
When just as I was plunging in a cloud
That lightened with the laugh of Hell and showed
It made of devilish faces which grew glad
And kindled at my coming, and all had
A gap-toothed wicked grin, as tho' each one
Saw in my face the kindred of his own,—

All the dark host rejoicing as I came ;
All making sure as Marksman of his aim,
When lo ! a Hawk swoops from its height unheard,
And from before his gun bears off his Bird !
So, while their claws for cruel welcome spread,
I was caught up ; borne swiftening overhead,
By one on wings of light, with lightning shod,
And then I knew that I was going to God ;
That life but sets in life still more profound,
As sunset into sunrise the world round ;
That all who enter by the gate of breath,
Must pass before the Awful eyes in death,
And stand all naked to the searching mien.
I could not shrivel away nor slink unseen !

" To me the vast and horrible Unknown
Was one dread face and all the face one frown !
Pain, sternness, pity eternal in a look
That read my life, wide-open as a book.
Not that the leaves turned over one by one
Revealing, page by page, all I had done,—
The Sense is as a scroll where manifold
Indelible things are day by day uprolled

And treasuried for the Memory to recall;
Maps of the mental world hung on the wall :
But Life is more than Letter or than Law,
And deftly as the brain may take or draw
Its daily tallies, never can it keep
In fixëd figure all the fathomless Deep
Of Consciousness conceals, whose restless sea
Ripples on changing sands unceasingly.
Spirit is one. It is the crystal book,
Clear thro' and thro', read at a single look.
To all the thoughts that ever passed thro' us
In life, in death we grow diaphanous.
We do not think what we have been, we ARE
Past, present, future, without near or far.
A glimpse of this is lightened, when the blind
Is raised, in drowning, from the seeing Mind !
So the electric flash, thrown on the wheel
Revolving swift in darkness, will reveal
Each whirling spoke distinct as standing still.
In spirit-world at once you find the whole
Of life contemporary with the soul.

" There is strange writing of the somewhile guest
Featured upon the form it leaves at rest,

Which men in some dim-wise may read, but here
Is the live Chronicler himself! the clear
Truth naked—brain and body were but dress—
Quickened by the Eternal consciousness.

" So, when before that face, I felt the frown,
There was no need of Hell to drag me down,
I could have welcomed wafts of burning flame
To clothe my nakedness of deadly shame.
I lifted to my brow one shading hand,
But snatched it burning from the Murderer's brand.
The other to mine eyes I pressed; 'twas red
And wet and dropping with the blood I shed.
I tried to cover up my aching sight
And found myself all eye to pitiless light.

" In olden times, it was the wont, they say,
To bring the Murderer where his victim lay,
And at his touch, as to his slaying knife,
The wound would flush . Death speak with lips of
        Life.

" So, from the frown, a golden-headed Child
Lookt out on me and innocently smiled !

" *I shrieked my guiltiness at sight of it,*
And downward plunged, for hiding in the Pit.

" 'Curse God and die,' *the Devil said of old.*
I curse, and back the curses crowd tenfold.
Against the cold Heaven strikes my burning breath,
To fall in drops of wrath, far worse than death.
And still I curse and still I cannot die ;
And still I watch for Death with pleading eye,
To find that he will nevermore draw nigh !
Would that the Mighty One had spit on me
And wiped the blot from his eternity !

PART III.

"MY *Temptress lives on still.*

She is a Wife
And Mother; lives an unsuspected life.
She hath grown fat and flourished on the ill,
The poison, that should naturally kill.
That cruel stain of Murder seemed to pass
From off her face of life as breath from glass.
I sometimes play the devil in her dream
And plague her with a glimpse, one lurid gleam
Of all my torment; her thick veil I tear
And lay the unholy of unholies bare,
Else were her heart untroubled, deaf and blind.
With her things out of sight are out of mind,
And should she hear a voice from the Unknown
She takes it for an echo of her own.

"*Ah, Mistress, did you know we have to stand*
Together yet, as equals, hand in hand,

Like Eve and Adam, chittering side by side,
Where not a leaf our nakedness can hide;
Our secret blazoned, as a flag unfurled
High_on the housetops of another world!

" She was a buxom beauty!   In her way
Imperious as the Thane's Wife in the Play.
A woman who upon the outside smiled,
Burnished like beetles, inwardly defiled;
With hair that like a thunder-cloud, black-
    brightening,
Caught the sunlight and flasht it back in lightning.
The Devil never toyed with worthier folds,
About a comelier throat, to strangle souls;
A face that dazzled you with life's white-heat,
Devouring, as it drew you off your feet,
With eyes that set the Beast o' the blood astir,
Leaping in heart and brain, alive for her;
Melted the sword of soul within its sheath:
The knee-joints loosened, smitten by her breath
Until you bowed, as the strong beast boweth,
When taken captive by the dark of death:
Lithe, amorous lips, cruel in curve and hue,
Which, greedy as the grave, my kisses drew

With hers, that to my mouth like live things clung
Long after, and in memory fiercely stung .
A dainty morsel of the Devil's meat
To roll beneath my tongue, as poison sweet !
Had not the Mother ate forbidden food,
This was the Daughter among Women that would.

" But what avails to cast on her the blame ?
I will not : will not name her by her name.
The deed is done ; the sin is sinned , the brand
Is on my brow ; the blood burns on my hand.

" I must have been a beast myself from birth.
We lived as Beasts in that old burrow of earth
They called a House; the Cot where I was born ;
One of those dwellings Poets will adorn
Outside with Honeysuckle and climbing Rose,
But where, within, no flower of Heaven blows
With sweetening breath, for want of air and light,
And in the wild weeds crawl the things of night :
Where any life-warmth quickens the dark slime
Of hovelled sin to swarm in shame and crime.

" My pastoral home was one wherein are grown
Boys for the Hulks; girls for the pitiless Town

That flaunts beneath the gaslights on the highway,
The full-blown flowers of many a filthy byeway!
Where Virtue had no safeguard, Vice no veil;
The Devil sowed his seed, never to fail—
With such a soil—in growing harvest meet
For him, as sure as corn is grown to eat.

" I should have been the beast that Nature binds
To beaten ways and with her blinkers blinds.
But, was a Beast with scope to work all ill;
Treat Wife and dumb things cruelly—sin—kill—
And go to Hell by freedom of the will.
And yet I knew not—such the curse of sin!—
Until the fall came, what was ripe within;
What demon I had nurst past suckling-time,
To find that he could go alone in crime.

" She came to me, her great black eyes aglare
Like stars of bale, yet with the hunted stare
Of wild things; such as made me stare to see
What danger followed her and threatened me.
I knew that Nemesis was drawing near,
And in the beating of my heart could hear
The hovering wings that bow strong men with fear.

D

'What is it?' *I asked.   What need for her to tell?*
'Twas writ all over her.   I knew too well.
And still I stared beyond, as if that way
The blackness rose that blotted out the day.
For days, and weeks, and months, her secret lay
Safe-nestled, unsuspected by her friends.
But one day all disguise in sinning ends,
And every way-side hiding-place is past.
She had to leave her home and fly at last—
Mad with the misery of a Mother's pain,
She ran to me, thro' fire, and hail, and rain,
And mire below, and thunder overhead;
Ran lightning-dazed, and drencht, till nearly dead.

" Well I remember that LAST DAY.   I see
It lightning-lit.   I feel it stamped in me,
As with the black seal of Eternity.
It was about mid-spring, when suddenly
The rear of beaten winter turned in ire,
And there was battle fierce of Frost and Fire.
The Birds stopped singing ; all the golden flame
O' the Sun went out; the Cattle homeward came.
With a forerunning shiver rusht the breeze,
And, in the Woods, the husht and listening trees,

That had been standing deathly-dark and still,
Wind-whitened sprang, with every leaf athrill.
I watched the anguisht clouds go hurrying by,
Rackt with the rending spirit of prophecy :
Like Pythonesses in the pangs, they tost
And writhed in shadowy semblance of the Lost :
They met, they darted death, they reared, they roared,
And down the torrent of the tempest poured !
Thro' heaven's windows the blue lightnings gleamed,
And like a fractured pane the sky was seamed :
Hailstones made winter on the whitened ground,
And for two hours the thunder warrayed round.
And then I heard the Thrush begin again,
With his more liquid warble after rain.

" Tearing thro' all the fearful storm she came ;
Worse storm within, and in her eyes hell-flame
Had broken loose to kindle, past control,
In huge dare-devilry of reckless soul.
As springs a Madman, dancing upon deck,
Who hath fired the Ship, and glories in the wreck ;
As at a Prison window one may stand
Who fired the house, and waves the lighted brand,

Her spirit sprang at me.   Her looks were wild.
She had come to me, she said, to bring the child,
For no one had a greater right to it !
This was God's truth, not merely meant for wit.
She swore that she had come there and would stay
Till it was born, and safely put away.
And even while I cursed her pangs grew worse,
And stopped me with an everlasting curse.

" 'Good God ! this is too bad,' *I thought; and laught*
A laugh as bitter as the cup I quaffed.
I had been married just a month ! my Wife
Knew nothing of this dead love come to life.
As Fate would have it, she had gone from home :
I knew that any hour she might have come.
With desperate voice the woman made me writhe,
Harsh as the whetstone on the Mower's scythe
She rasped me all on edge; the hell-sparks flew,
Till there seemed nothing that I dared not do.
'Kill it, you Coward !   Why not kill us both ? '
She taunted me; and I felt little loth.
The Devil whispered 'Why not kill them both ? '
I said I would, and clenched it with an oath."

Now, while he spake, there came a frightful
    change
Upon him with transfiguration strange,
And slowly he assumed his mortal dress
With a last look of dying consciousness :
The eyes turned stony in a sightless stare,
And of all presence he grew unaware :
Clouded and lost within his dreadful dream
He went ; a Man once more, each pore a stream
Of inner agony ; his body shook,
And from his mazëd face did " MURDER " look.
It was as when in dreams you see a dumb
Mouth shaped to cry it, tho' no sound will come.
While in his hand he grasped a gleaming knife,
So keen, you saw it thirst for a drink of life !
And, as he passed into his haunted gloom,
His dreadful purpose drew him from the room.

So terrible the scene, I should have cried
For help in the death-eddies,—must have died
But for the strong calm Spirit at my side,
Who took me by the hand and turned on mine
His cordial face with comfortable shine.

And then the darkness gave a sudden sigh,
And a wind rose that went lamenting by.
" *Listen*," he said.   I leaned, all ear, to hark ;
I felt the quake of footsteps thro' the dark,
Heavily hurrying down a distant stair,
And caught a piteous wail faint on the air.
The Dog howled his lone cry, as he would fain
Give warning, knowing it was all in vain.
Then came the liquid gurgle and the ring
Metallic, with the heavy plop and ping,
Heavier than largest water-drops that fall
From melting icicles on house-eaves tall.
I knew them now ; this resurrection night
Sounds were translated into things of sight.
These were the innocent drops a father shed.
They had the weight of blood, fell heavy as lead.
And now again I felt the grinding sound
O' the grating door ; the digging underground ;
The shudders of the house ; the sighs and moans ;
The ring of iron dropped upon the stones ;
The cloudy presence groping near ; the quake
Of walls that vibrate with the parting shake ;
Then the relief.   As they who stoop with dread,
While the Simoom goes withering overhead

Like iron red-hot, look up and breathe at last,
So felt I when that thing of Night had passed.

'Tis but a dream, methought, and I shall wake
Ere long and from its dread embraces break.
And if I could but only wake, I knew
By light of day these things could not be true!
How many a dream before had wraith-like gone
To nothing at the sceptic smile of Dawn.
And still I could not wake, nor wake my Wife;
And still the dream went on, and like as life
There stood the Angel in it; overshone
The well-known room.
     And then the voice went on.

" *The nether world hath opened at your feet,*
And you have seen ascending from the Pit
The torment-smoke, where furnace-fires of Crime
Have crackt the crust of this your world of Time.

" *It was an awful hour of storm and rain*
And starless gloom in which the Child was slain.
Wild, windily the Night went roaring by,
As if loud seas broke in the woodlands nigh,

Or all the blasts of Heaven at once were hurled
To stop the onward rolling of the world.
The firmament was all one flash, and red
The lightning laught, as Hell were overhead.

" He had dug his grave amid this war of storm.
He bore the murdered Babe upon his arm
For burial, where no eye should ever mark.
Just then Heaven opened at him with the bark
Of all the Hell-hounds loosed.   And in the dark
Out went the light, and down he dropt the key,
That was to lead to safety secretly.
He was alone with Death, and paces three
Beyond the door an open grave gaped, free
For all the daylight world to come and see ;
And he was fastened.

                Like the luckless wight
Who wagered he would enter a Vault at night
In some old Graveyard, and, in proof he did,
Would leave his dagger stuck in a Coffin-lid.—
He ventured : bravely dasht the weapon down
And turned to triumph, when, by the student gown
He was held fast, as if the living tomb
Had closed upon him, clutched him in the gloom.

He had pinned his long robe to the coffin !   Fright
Came on him like a snow-fall !   Weirdly-white
His hair turned, and the youth was a forlorn,
Old, grey-faced, gibbering Idiot next morn.

" *The Murderer did not madden thus, but he*
Was stamped that moment for Eternity.
He stooped with his dead child, he groped and found
The key, and got the corse safe underground,
And out of sight had hid his murder-hole,
Ere Dawn lookt ghostly on his guilty soul,
And on his hands no man could see the stain.
His madness went beyond the burning brain,
His was the frenzy of a soul insane.

" *The hour came when he lost the key again.*
As the death-rattles thundered in his throat,
And earth was rushing past his soul afloat,
And pain had fiercely throbbed itself to rest,
And Time stopped ticking in the brain and breast,
It gleamed and vanisht from his fading sight,
And snapped his eye-strings straining thro' the night.

Thenceforth it was his hottest hell to be
Living the moment when he lost that key :
Hell that is permanent insanity !

" There was a man who died ages ago,
And 'tis his madness still to wile his woe
At work for ever, perfecting the plan
That should have, must have shown his fellow-man
How innocent he was of that old crime
He died for justly—had he thought in time.

" Even so this lost soul whirls and eddies round
The grave-place where the lost key must be found,
If the mad motion would a moment cease
And he could only get a moment's peace ;
He often sees it, but he cannot touch
It ; like a live thing it eludes his clutch—
Gone like that glitter from the eyes of Death
In the black river at night that slides beneath
The Bridges, tempting souls of Suicides
To find the promised rest it surely hides.

" For seven years it was his curse to come
At midnight and fulfil his dreadful doom,

Looking for that lost key, lest it revealed
The secret he so cunningly concealed ;
Feeling at times he could endure his hell
If in one world of torment he might dwell.
And still from world to world he had to go
(A rootless weed the wave swings to and fro !)
Wandering with incommunicable woe ;
Well knowing that, for every moment lost,
His soul would be in treble anguish tost,
While every storm of wind and rain would
    beat
Down on him, kindle hell to tenfold heat,
And make him hurry to your upper air,
Lest it should blow and wash the bones all bare.
For often will a wind of God arise
At midnight, and the voice of Murder cries
From it, and bones of murdered babes are found ;
Earth will no longer be their burial ground.
And so on stormy nights his pangs are worst :
More dread the gnashings of that soul accurst.

" For seven years he came, unseen, unheard.
'Twas but the other day the bones were stirred,

As men were delving heedless underground.
They broke in on them, scattered them around :
Not guessing they were human.

                            Lower in hell

His spirit sank, like waters in a well
Before there springs the Earthquake.   Tremblings
    sore
Shook him with vengeance never felt before.
He came ; he found the murder had leaped out ;
The grave was burst ; the bones were strewn about
For all the world to find !

                       It mattered not

To him that no one knew them ; they might rot
To undistinguishable dust in peace ;
That Death had signed his order of release
From this world's law, Death had no shadows
    dim
Enough to hide the blacker truth from him.
He was the Murderer still, who had to hide
The proofs of murder on the human side !
The Child was his ; these were its tender bones,
Blown with the dust and dasht against the stones.
And all his care, his self-enfolded pain
And midnight watchings lone, were all in vain.

" *The worms that in the dead flesh riot and roll*
Are poor faint types of those that gnawed his soul!
For ever beaten now; tho' he should find
And grasp the key he lost when he went blind
In death: in vain he mounts upon a wind
Of hell and tries to fan the dry dust over them
With endless toil; no sooner may he cover them
Than there's an ominous muttering in the air,
And in an instant all the bones lie bare;
While lurking devils grin thro' masks at him,
In likeness of his Child's head, gorily grim!

" *It comes upon him, almost with a gleam*
Of comfort, when he's rapt into the Dream
You saw him change in, and he passes thro'
His night of murder; lives it all anew,
So vividly each sound is heard by you;
Each particle of Matter set afloat
Upon a Mind-wave, tossing like a boat
The Spirit rides.

   For, as, upon his brain,
The sounds one midnight smote in a ruddy rain,
Till sense had dyed the spirit with their stain,
And Memory was branded deep as Cain,

So now his spirit echoes back again
The fixed ideas of a soul insane,
Till Matter taking impress of his pain,
Reverberates the sounds within your brain."

PART IV

I MUSED and mused in great astonishment,
 While on, and on, the growing wonder went
Within, without, on wings that widelier spread.
" *How many things* " oft to myself I had said,
" *I have to ask, if one came from the dead.*"
And now I had my wish. My thought could rise
No fleeter than the answer filled his eyes
And flasht electric utterance with the whole
Illumined figure of a living soul !
And, ere I shaped my question, what was dim
And dumb in me shone clear as light in him.

" *More Laws than Gravitation keep us down*
To the old place from whence the soul had flown.
Not every one in death can get adrift
Freely for life. Some have no wings to lift

Their weary weight : the body of their sin
Which they so evilly have laboured in.
Others will touch as 'twere the window-sill
To flutter back upon the ground-floor still.
Others yet grovel like the beast belogged
In the old ways, to which they are self-clogged.
Just as the spirits of an earlier race
Of Man in dwarfhood, kept their dwelling-place
On earth, and revelling in the moon's pale rays,
Were seen as Wee Folk in old wondering days.

" A-many wander this side of the grave
To get the last glimpse they can ever have
Of those they loved, who will be lost in light,
While they go darkling and are lost in night.
They see them sometimes in the world of breath ;
They part for ever at the second death.
Others would blot from out the book of Time
The published proofs of their long-secret crime
That glare so guiltily to spirit sight.
Teachers who called Good evil; darkness light;
Who see more clearly in the unclouding day,
Strive to recall the souls they led astray,

And find the world, that once hung on their breath,
Goes by them now, heedless and deaf as Death.
Some, who have done a wrong that, unperceived,
Ran to a sea of sin, are sorely grieved,
And ready to spend a life-time shut from bliss,
Might they but right the wrong they did in this :
So clear, so awful, when the past is seen,
Grows the dark mystery of might-have-been.

" You know the Mill upon the windy hill,
That stands all day so desolate and still ;
The weary, dreary, dark, deserted Mill,
Whose loneliness doth all the horizon fill,
With outspread arms appealing to the sky
And one dim window like a blinded eye ?
I see those long arms tossing thro' the night,
While from the window gleams unearthly light
Which furtive forms will dimly flit before,
With feet that stir no dust upon the floor.
These are the Ghosts of those who robbed the Poor
In old dead years !   And now, by window and door,
We catch their faces, wearing such a look
Of prayer as Men have when a ship has struck.

E

But no one comes to take his own again,
And there is none to ease them of their pain.
Repentance woke so late, their toil is vain,
Night after night upon the haunted hill
In that old desolate, doom-stricken Mill.

" This happened beneath the broad shining day,
Right in the rush of life that makes its way
Thro' London streets.
                    Slowly, mid that swift throng,
A thoughtful man went mooningly along;
More lonely in that wilderness of men.
And at a corner where the Devil's den
Is palace-fronted now— all gilt and glass—
Illuminating nightly all who pass
By the broad way to hell with gin and gas,
And souls are sloughed, like city sewage,
     down
Dead-seaward, thro' the sink-holes of the town,
He heard a pitiful voice that took strange hold
Of him; ran thro' his blood in lightnings cold;
Mournful, remote, and hollow, as if the tomb
Had buried a live spirit in its gloom,

Monotonously sounding on below
A vast unutterable weight of woe;
A voice that its own speaker would not know!
As if unbreathing life were doomed to bear
Shut down on it the load of all the air.
He stopped.

    A woman clothed in rags he saw
With fixed beseeching eyes begin to draw
Him to her; left no power to say them nay.
With one stretcht arm she begged; on the other lay,
Soft in a snow of gold, a Cherub Child!
So have you seen a Glowworm on the wild
Bleak moorland; all the dusk a moment smiled.

" For the babe's sake he thrust a coin of gold
Into her hand! but, it fell thro', and rolled
Ringing along the stones: he followed, found
It, brought it back and lookt around:
There was no woman waiting with her hand
Outstretcht, no Child, where he had seen them
  stand.
In vain he searched each by-way round about;
Thro' life even, never made the mystery out.

" *The truth is, he was one of those who see*
At times side-glimpses of eternity.
The Beggar was a Spirit, doomed to plead
With hurrying wayfarers, who took no heed,
But passed her by, indifferent as the dead,
Till one should hear her voice and turn the head;
Doomed to stand there and beg for bread, in tears,
To feed her child that had been dead for years!
This was the very spot where she had spent
Its life for drink, and this the punishment;
Feeling she had let it slip into the grave,
And now would give eternal life to save:
Heartless and deaf and blind the world went by,
Until this Dreamer came, with seeing eye;
The good Samaritan of souls had given
And wrought the change that was to her as Heaven.

" *It is not Crime alone brings Spirits back*
To pull beside you in the wonted track.
Shadows of mortal care will cloud the brow
That should have shone as clear as sunlit snow:
And those who hindered here must help you now.
Not always can the soul forgive in heaven
Itself for deeds that God hath long forgiven.

" *A wedded couple, bedded, snug as birds*
In nested peace, one night must needs have words
Of strife before they slept.   A foolish thing
Had on a sudden set them bickering;
Some wild-fire wisp had dropt a subtle spark
That kindled at a breath blown thro' the dark,
And all their passion burst in tongues of flame :
Their anger blinding each to personal blame.
She had been pillowed on his beating heart,
And in an instant they had sprung apart !
The arm that wound about her he withdrew,
And Night, with dark divorce, came 'twixt the
    two.

" *A little thing had plucked them palm from palm ;*
A little thing had broke their happy calm ;
A little thing fall'n in the pleasant path
Of their life-stream, that turned to bubbling wrath !
And little might have made them yield and cling
Repentant ; yea, a very little thing.
A touch would have sufficed to make the stream
Flow free once more ; dream out its happy dream.
A kiss have fused them into one again,
And saved them many a year of piteous pain.

'Twas such a little thing they had to do;
Both yearned to make it up, and this both knew.
If one could but have said 'Good night,' scared Love
Would have come down to brood like Holy Dove.
And, being done, all would have been so well.
Not being done, it left the rift for Hell
To break thro', and another triumph win.
Ever the worst of Traitors are within.
But neither spoke, tho' long upon the wing
Love waited lingeringly listening!

" Waking, he heard her in her slumbers weep,
And then he slept, and in the guise of Sleep
Death came for him, nor gave him time to say
' Good night,' ' Good-bye,' and at his side she lay
A Widow! And upon that dark no day
Hath broke for her. For him, nor hell nor heaven
Will open; praying still to be forgiven,
Night after night at her bedside he stands,
Wringing his soul as one may wring the hands;
By natural law of grievèd love; not sent
In vengeance and unnatural punishment.

" *The unslain shadows of the Martyrs slain,*
Rise on their fields of old heart-ache and pain,
To fight their battle over and over again.
Half-buried hands, still thrust up thro' the sod,
From fields of carnage, prayerfully to God,
Will grasp the weapons of immortal war.
Freed spirits make their conquering battle-car
Of human hearts: they did but hold their breath
To smite unheard in their dark cloud of death.
They work for Freedom still, tho' out of sight;
They are torch-bearers in your mortal night.
The Tyrants may destroy the body, drench
The life out with the blood, but cannot quench
The spirit, nor put out the awful light
O' the stars that in their courses 'gainst them fight!

" *Wide as the wings of Sleep by night are spread,*
Are Freedom's Exiles scattered, and her dead
Have lain their bodies down 'neath God's great dome.
But every banisht spirit hurries home,
Soon as the free, long-fettered life upsprings
Awave one day on mighty warrior-wings.
Each soul, let out, fights with the strength of seven,
Under God's shield, and on the side of heaven.

" *The secret meaning of the marvels told*
Of wars in heaven and visions seen of old,—
When, with a fiery cloud of witnesses,
The other world made its dumb-show to this
And drew vast plans of battle on the air,
Alive with death and lit with vengeful glare,—
Was, that the heavens on their huge scroll unfurled
The imagery of war in spirit world;
Reflecting, on the ceiling of the night,
The shadowy forms embattled beyond sight.

" *The other world is not cut off from this :*
Forgetfulness is not the gate of bliss.
At times the buried dead within you rise
To look out on their old world through your eyes ;
They touch you with the waving of their wing,
Lightly as airs of heaven the Æolian string.
At times as Comforters above you stoop,
To lift the burden from you when ye droop !
As parents on their little ones may peep
Ere going to rest, they bend to bless your sleep.
With fruit from our Lord's Garden dear ones
     come
To bring ye a foretaste ; try to lure you home.

" *With clap o' the shoulder, friends behind you steal*
The old glad way, tho' ye no longer feel :
They watch you as ye watch the darkened mind
Of some arrested spirit ; try to unwind
A way to it ; with drops of pity melt
The clod about it ; have your fondness felt !
Even as ye turn your thoughts to them above,
Do they return to you ; look back for love.

" *They left you standing still at gaze upon*
The cloud they entered, where the light last shone.
And while the wet eyes watch, and wait, and yearn,
As if by that same way they might return,
And through the dark ye stretch the ungrasped hand,
There, at some window of the soul, they stand
All whitely clothed with immortality,
Closer to you than flesh and blood can be.

" *Old loves are with you in your dreams ; but fear*
Lest they should make their presence felt too near ;
The face of Love in Heaven they dare not show ;
For with its glory they might set aglow
Your earthly love, which leaps to embrace a bliss
That lives and dies in a consuming kiss.

So warm Laodamïa wooed her dead
Dear Husband's Shade, as if they were new wed!

" And certain spirits are perplexed to find
How like their life to that they left behind
In natural nearness to their darlings here,
Who lose them just because they are so near
In life that grows impenetrably clear!

" Many that tossed together on the sea,
And parted in the storm; lost utterly;
Find they were only wreckt to meet again,
Safe on the same shore, after all the pain.
God hath so many ways by which we come
To Him; through many a door He draws us
      Home.

" Others are horribly startled at the change
Revealed in death, all is so ghastly strange!
So many Masters in the realms of breath
Serve at the feet of those who are crowned in
      death.
So many weeds, your blind world flung aside,
Are gathered up as flowers, thrice glorified.

The Invisible dawns !   The sleepers wake to find
Less death in dying than in living blind :
And now the eyes their earthy scales let fall,
They see that they have never lived at all.

" I've known a follower of the strictest faith,
Whose dead religion rested on a death,
And frequent praying in the market-place,
With proclamation of his private grace ;
Who sat among the loftiest Self-Elect,
But had not learned through life to walk erect—
Strait-waistcoated in stony pieties—
And when Death came—the Iconoclast who frees—
He could not stand without their rigid stay.
The Maker's image had but stamped the clay.
On earth he wore the mask of Man awhile,
But when the Searchers, with their slow, calm
  smile,
Had stripped him, the soul shrank from man's
  disguise:
It fled, and fell, and wriggled, reptile-wise.

" I've seen the foolish slaves of luxury,
Who loll at ease and live deliciously ;

In Pleasure's poppy-garden drowse and press
With amorous arms my Lady Idleness;
Who, floating downward in voluptuous dream,
Just lean to catch the sparkles from Life's stream
That runs with Siren-sound and dizzying dance,
And hides its wrecks with winking radiance,—
Who, risen from life's feast, came reeling thence
Immortals, drunken with the fumes of Sense;
I've seen them in a pleasure-seeking group,
At Death's low door with mock politeness stoop,
And wantonly they went, nodding the head,
As tho' to lightsome music they were led :
Heedless the merry madcaps came before
The awful gate, as 'twere a Playhouse door.
It opened, and the darlings entered in
As to the secret Paradise of Sin !
But in a moment what a change there was.
In front of them there rose a mocking glass
In place of drop-scene—this was not a Play—
In which they stared, and could not turn away,
But still stared on, in silence one and all,
To see their finery fade, their feathers fall ;
In which grim moulting of the plumes of pride
They had to lay all ornaments aside ;

And on the face of every Woman and Man,
Like wet paint on a mask, the colours ran;
The skin grew writhled, and within the head
Their eyes lookt like grey ghosts of hopes long dead.

" The naked image of their own selves they see,
Stripped in the mirror of eternity;
Worm-eaten through and through with thoughts that
    prey
On life itself and rot the soul away.
Wine-cups await them; though well-kept for years
The wine, it had been made of human tears,
And tasted bitter! Fruit was given to eat,
The fruit of their own life; so smiling-sweet
It lookt! like Apples when the shining round
Is made of rose-leaf on a golden ground;
The crimson and the golden melting thro',
Right to the core, in one delicious hue.
But these were Apples of the Dead-Sea shore;
Ashes without, and maggots at the core.
Saluting their fine nostrils Odours rise;
The scent of lifelong human sacrifice!
The brother's blood, that climbs to them and
    cries.

Then are they led where healing waters wait
To wash the soilèd soul; repristinate
The image of God so earthily concealed;
But while they lave find, more and more revealed,
Deeper disfigurement and deadlier stain,
As wetted marble shows the darker grain.

PART V.

"THE *dim world of the dead is all alive;*
    All busy as the bees in summer hive;
More living than of old; a life so deep,
To you its swifter motion looks like sleep.
Whether in bliss they breathe, in bale they
    burn,
His own eternal living each must earn.
We suck no honeycomb in drowsy peace,
Because ennobling natural cares all cease;
We live no life, as many dream, caressed
By some vast lazy sea of endless rest—
For there, as here, unbusy is unblest.

"*Man is the wrestling-place of Heaven and*
    Hell,
Where, foot to foot, Angel and Devil dwell,
With both attractions drawing him. *This gives*
The perfect poise in which his freedom lives.

No one so near to heaven to lack for scope;
No one so near to hell to lose all hope.
Whichever way he wills, to left or right,
Lets in a flood of supernatural might.
He flames out hellward, and all hell is free,
Rejoicing in the gust of liberty,
To rush in on him, work its devilry!
In strength of faith, or feebleness of fear,
He bows and bends the highest heavens near.
The brightness upon Prayer's uplifted face
Reflects some spirit-presence in the place.

" Each impure nature hath its parasites,
That live and revel in unclean delights.
Like moths around a flame they swim and swarm,
Or flies about a horse, that ride the warm
And reeking air which is their atmosphere,
Their breath of life, the ranker the more dear.
They glory in the grossness of the blood,
For, reptile-like, they lay their eggs in mud.
In every darksome corner of the mind
They hang their webs, the wingèd life to bind;
Weaving the shadow of the Evil One
To darken 'twixt the spirit and its sun.

" *If those blind Unbelievers did but know*
Thro' what a perilous Unknown they go
By night and day; what furtive eyes do mark
Them fiercely from their ambush of the dark;
What motes of spirit dance in every beam;
What grim realities mix with their dream;
What serpents try to pull down fallen souls,
As earth-worms drag the dead leaves through their
     holes;
What cunning sowers drop the seed by night
That flames to fatal flower in broad daylight;
What foul birds drop their eggs in innocent
     nests,
To win their heat from warmth of innocent breasts:
What snaky thieves o'ermount each garden wall;
On life's fresh leaves what caterpillars crawl;
What cool green pleasaunces and brooding bowers
Are set with soul-traps hid among the flowers;
What Tempters in the Chamber of Sleep will break,
And with insidious whisperings keep awake
The Soul! How, toad-like, at the ear will lurk
The cunning Satan, wickedly at work:
What evil spirits hover in amorous hate
Round him who nibbles at the devil's bait,

F

Or him who dallies, fingering the sharp edge
Of peril, or sits with feet over the ledge,
By some dark water, with his face ash-wan,
Until they urge him over; a doomed Man!
What cruel demons try to break a way,
Thro' weak brains, back to the lost world of day,
And from some little rift in nature yawns
A black abysm of madness, and Hell dawns:
What starvelings seek to drink Corruption's breath
From rosy life, more rich than rot of death;
What ghosts of drinkers old would quench their
    drouth
At the wine-bibber's dreaming stertorous mouth;
What Sirens seek to kindle at your fire
Of passion some live spark of dead desire—
They would be ready even to doubt God's power
To shield their little life from hour to hour,
And many would be going, with idiot-grin,
Out of their mind to let the marvel in.

" But do not think the Devil hath his will.
Whate'er he doth he is God's servant still.
And in the larger light of day divine
The spark of his hell-fire shall cease to shine.

God maketh use of him ; what he intends
For evil Heaven will shape to its own ends.
With subtle wile he tries to circumvent
The Lord, and works just what the Master meant.
He hangs the dark cloud round this world of yours ;
God smileth, and a rain of good down-pours.
He dug Christ's tomb so deep there sprang and
swirled
Waters of life to baptize all the world.
He strove to found the Empire of the Slave,
It crumbled in : he had but delved its grave.

" He stole upon a Nation, in disguise
Of thieves that prowled by night ; day-lurking spies ;
Plotters who privily set their eyes to mark
Her weakness, and garrotted her by dark !
The face of Freedom frightfully they scarred,
That men should know her not, so sadly marred,
And, seeing her in the dust, misjudge her stature ;
And, finding she grew calm, mistake her nature !
They built about her ; dreamed not she would stand
Up, terribly tall once more ; and, in her hand—
Clencht, till the knuckles whiten with their grip—
The sword set sharp as is her red-edged lip :

And in her eyes the lightnings that should break
In blinding, black, irreparable wreck :—
Rending their roof to heaven, their walls to earth,
(The sorer travail the more glorious birth!)
An Earthquake crash! the edifice is crowned,
And there's a heap of ruin on the ground!
Arise, to sweep them from her onward path,
Stern as the Spectre of God's whitest wrath.
Even while they clutcht the gains of their foul play
And parted them, I heard the Avengers say—
'They plant in dust a breath will blow away,
Altho' they wet it well with blood to-day.

" 'Ay, Traitor, mount your topmost pinnacle.
The merry-making Heavens would mark you well,
Where all the gazers of the world may see
You throned upon the peak of infamy!'
So croon'd the implacable ministers of Fate,
Standing in shadow where they watch and wait.

" 'Well done. Now place the crown upon your brow,
With its brave glitter all eyes dazzle now :
Lost in its splendour is that frightful stain
Branded beneath ; the murder-mark of Cain!'

So croon'd the implacable ministers of Fate,
Standing in shadow where they watch and wait.

" 'Well done. Now fold the Imperial Purple round,
And let a Pope's Anointed, robed and crown'd,
Thus glorify the blood so basely spilt ;
Thus image to all time the loftiest guilt.'
So croon'd the implacable ministers of Fate,
Standing in shadow where they watch and wait.

" ' Well done, thou faithful servant. Hell shall rise
From half her thrones to offer you their prize,
And greet your coming ; meet you with a kiss
Of benison, for such a deed as this !'
So croon'd the implacable ministers of Fate,
Standing in shadow where they watch and wait."

" Was Satan sent from heaven to ruin earth ? "
I asked, " or what the story of his birth ? "

" *Both heaven and hell are from the human race,*
And every soul projects its future place :
Long shadows of ourselves are thrown before,
To wait our coming on the eternal shore.

These either clothe us with eclipse and night,
Or, as we enter them, are lost in light.

" There is no Devil such as Milton saw ;
No fallen Angel's eyes divined the flaw
In God's work, whereby Man might be accurst.
The Devil was a murderer from the first,
Our Saviour said.   But he was softly nurst
Up from a babe in arms.   A little seed
Of sin was sown that grew with little heed.
By door or window little sins will win
A way that widens for the larger sin,
As tiniest lichens, climbing up the wall,
May lend a hand to help the Ivy crawl
That is to tower a conqueror over all
The house in ruin, crumbling to the fall.
Once life is set in motion there upspring
Infinite issues to the smallest thing.
A finger's breadth in swerving as we start
May land us in the end two worlds apart.

" Our parents were not tempted by a Tree
That hung out luscious fruitage, visibly

Held in God's hand, on purpose to beguile
Their simpleness with its suggesting smile.
That is the symbol of a world within ;
There was the serpent born, there bred the sin.
The trees that midmost in the Garden stood,
Took root in soul and blossomed in the blood.
Nor were they left without the inward light,
The starry presence shining thro' your night,
That shows the wrong while it reveals the right :
The magnet in the soul that points on thro'
All tempests and still trembles to be true.

" The still small voice within cried

       ' Do not this

Or it will lead from me, and ye will miss
The innocent brightness of your morning bliss,
And long in a wild wilderness will stray,
Farther and farther from the primal way,
Until ye lose me, darkling in a cloud
Of your own making, winding like a shroud
About the life I gave ; nor feel me near
When ye do call and think there's none to hear.'

" And yet they dallied with the thought of wrong
Until they did it : looking down too long,

Like him who, on a perilous mountain ledge,
Gazes upon the gulf, dark o'er the edge,
Till he grows dizzy and, with brain a-swim,
Forgetting to look up—drops ! Or, like him
Who stood and watched that Titan, face to face,
The vast Steam-Hammer, with its monster mace,
Until the blows of its recurrent sound
Snapped his last trembling hold on things around ;
Mazed him and drew him nigher, slip by slip,
To thrust his hand into its crushing grip.

" They dallied with wrong-doing, and it grew
Too strong to wrestle with, and overthrew.
Eyes play with Pleasure ! Looking overmuch
Sets all the blood a-tingle for the touch !
How the fruit smiles, delicious to the eyes ;
How quietly the Snake behind it lies,
With all his weight bending the branch down
        near ;
The reptile music, sliding thro' the ear,
Winds round the soul, makes it a-tiptoe stand
With love-sick longing till it lifts the hand
To pluck, and feel, and smell, and taste just one
Ripe Apple, whose gold glistens so i' the sun !

But one step over the forbidden marge;
The sin so little, the delight so large!
And there's the old, old story of the Fall,
Eternally repeated for us all.

" Thus is the Devil born: born every day,
Harmless at first as toothless whelps at play;
Is born in thoughts which are the quick live
   seeds
That will be striving to take shape in deeds:
So would be born did any Pair begin
Afresh; so form the protoplasm of Sin,
The pustule raised at just a prick of pin;
The nest-egg which the Devil is hatched in.
For Man, the outcome of Creation's past,
Is flower of all earth's life from first to last:
No lower life hath ever passed away
But left its larvæ in the human clay.
No reptile of the slime, no beast of prey,
But human passions personate to-day.
And these break loose to rend in deadly strife,
And will break loose, till, in the higher life,
The soul arisen to her immortal stature
Leads, Una-like, these grim necessities of Nature.

" *The sin that sprang, equipped for death, in Cain,*
Was gathering life for many years ; had lain
In childhood nestled to the parent breast,
Who dreamed not of the wild beast he caressed
So gently ; fed on his own life, with pride,
The strength that gored him in mad fratricide !
Such little sins are fibres to the root
Of that which bears ripe murder for its fruit.

" *To picture what I mean : see here, a Wife,*
With bosom just a-brood o'er life-in-life,
Who in a fury-fit snatched up a knife
And drove it at her husband. 'Twas a miss
Tho' near enough to hear Death's arrow hiss !
She had not dyed her hand in human blood,
But she had dipped her Unborn in a flood
Of wrath that surged and smoked and flashed hell-flame ;
Given her babe baptism in the Devil's name :
Stained the pure thing of heaven a lurid hue
With fume o' the pit, the white star reddened thro'.
And from that Mother-stricken life there grew
A Murderer whose own hand that Mother slew.

" *The ghosts of our own crimes long-buried will*
Live after us and haunt our children still.

Our vices, hid for generations past,
Break out and tell their secret tale at last.

" Cain slew his brother.   In that deed the Devil
Took visible shape ; stood forth erect, as Evil
Full-statured, from the serpent form of sin
In which he had wormed a way and wriggled in,
Before he got a foothold on the earth.

" The Murderer died, and spirit-world gave birth
To a thing that stained the stainless in a cloud
So black it made the clear heaven thunder-browed ;
Death at the heart, Destruction on the wing !
This was the spirit of Cain, still hovering
Over the world, to rain in ruin down.
So Tyrants climb to wear the fatal crown
That sets them on a vantage-ground, to tread
A people's life out—deal death overhead.

" From Earth sprang Satan, clothed with plumes of
        power.
But, as a Bird, in the death-pangs, will tower
To fall, his exultation dropped to see
The loneliness of his eternity !

The old world-wall no longer hemmed him round ;
The Boundless was his spirit's only bound ;
The conscious stillness ached upon the ear ;
No breath of being stirring far or near.
A Waste no wing had wandered, foot had trod
No print upon ; a world left out by God.
And he the only life-beat of the whole
Illimitable solitude of soul.

" What wonder he should turn to Earth again
And feel his way back to the human ; fain
To win a partner that would share his pain ?

" The worst of Devils feel a little ease,
Shedding their poison ; giving their disease
To uninfected souls.   And soon he saw
How he might take advantage of the Law
That seems to work so blindly, while Men draw
Their lots as blindly ; lets the sunshine fall
On just and unjust : gives one chance for all,
Nor spares the innocent when the guilty fall ;
How beauty broods with its thrice-glorious glow
Where Death is lurking quietly below !
How Providence looks on the side of Wrong
Nine times in ten if it be only strong :

How unperceived God works by common light,
Nor cleaves his cloud to lighten through our night;
How much Man has to trust Him—even for breath
To feed his life and faith to live through death.
Rare mischief may be done ere God appears
Himself in miracle.   He so often hears
The cry unanswered, save in His own way
And season.   Here was scope enough to play
The devil with the appearances of things;
Keep out of sight and pull the puppet-strings.

" And, at the thought, he waved abroad his wings
For larger flight, to spread himself between
Man and his Maker; weave his web unseen,
Right in the dazzle of the heavenly light;
Beat down the prayers and yearnings in mid-flight;
Make shadows in the mind to curtain day
From the dim world in which poor wretches stray:
Put out in tears the trembling inner ray
And lure them with a Will-o'-the-wisp at play
Among the quagmires waiting by the way;
Ventriloquise the voice of God within
The soul and in a guise Angelic win
From Heaven, by mirroring that heaven in

Death's stream; make spirits take the leap for love
Of that false reflex of the beauty above!

" First Man-Slayer, He reached his ghastly goal,
And then became first slayer of the soul.

" And doing evil grew a dear delight,
And so he built his kingdom of the night
And proudly waxed in power; his business thrived;
For soon the Murderer with a Murderess wived,
Whom he had wooed in secret many a day
And dragged at last along the same by-way,
To share with him the same blood-guilty fate,
And with fit offspring crown the loves of Hate.

" The Devil is no more the single soul
Of that first Murderer; it is the whole
Vast aggregate of evil spirits lost;
The cruel wreckers on that hell-bound coast.
Just as the person of the Holy Ghost
May mean the presence of a heavenly Host!
Or as ye say one spirit moves them when
One cry awakens from ten thousand men.

PART VI.

"THIS world is not the Devil's merry-go-round.
  The Angels of the Lord are ever found
Encamped about the soul that looks to Him :
They are an inner lamp when all is dim
Without, and light poor souls thro' horrors grim.
Even as a myriad sunbeams hour by hour
Melt to make rich one little summer flower ;
Or as a myriad souls of flowers fleet
Away to make a single summer sweet—
So many spirits make one smile of God
That feeds your life transfiguring from its clod.
There is no lack of Angel carriers
When mortals post to God their fervent prayers !
And these are happy in their work, for still
They find their heaven in doing the Father's will.
I have a meat, said Christ, ye know not of.
So these—they carry heaven in their love.

Not that the Blessëd leave their happy seat
When they draw near ye upon silent feet.
They do not need to thread their starry way
Through worlds of night, or wilderness of day.
Spirit to Spirit hath not far to run,
Because in God all souls are verily one
Throughout all worlds : there are no walls of Space
Where all eternity is dwelling-place.

" Distance is nothing in the world of Thought ;
And in the world of Spirit it is nought.
You hear of dying men whose souls have been
Present with distant friends ; most surely seen
Before the breathing ceased ; for they were there
In Thought so fixed, intense, that, on the air,
Their lineaments the utter yearning wrought,
In spiritual apparition of their thought,
Till they grew visible.   This Murderer dwells
In Spirit where his Thought is—hottest Hell's
For him where his infernal deed was done !
The blood so safely hidden from the sun
Hath stained right through beyond this world of
*   time,*
Red to the other side, with his old crime.

He does not merely come and go ; he is
All presence to the proofs and witnesses.

" Spirits may touch you, being, as you would say,
A hundred thousand million miles away.
Those wires that wed the Old World with the
    New,
Are not the only links Mind lightens thro' !
The Angels, singing in their heaven above,
Feel when ye strike the unison of love.
The prayers of heaven fall in a blessëd rain,
On souls that parch in purgatorial pain.
And prayers from earth lift, with a sense of wings,
Poor souls that drift as helpless outcast things.

" A luminiferous ether of the soul
Pervades the universe, and makes the whole
Vast realm of Being one ;—all breathing breath
Of the same life that is fulfilled in death.
And human spirits, from their earthy bound,
Can thrill the Immortals, in their crystal round,
Like flames that rise and answer a sweet sound :
And set the farthest heavens vibrating,
As air will dance close to a live harpstring.

G

" *Thus Jesus warned you that His Little Ones—*
Nestled like smallest planets next their Suns—
Are nearest God's great Angels, whose high place
Permits them to behold the Father's face,
With whom there is no distance known to sense.
Heaven is most near to utmost innocence.

" *God, the Creator, doth not sit aloof,*
As in a picture painted on the roof,
Occasionally looking down from thence.
He is all presence and all providence; •
Sentient in whatsoever life may draw
Breath from Him, and, beyond, sentient in law.
He doth not sit at one end of the chain
Of Being, thrilling it now and again;
He who is Being and doth bound and bind
Its particles in the Eternal Mind.
Outside His providence we cannot stand.
His presence makes the smallest room expand
Wider than wings of Day and Night e'er fanned.
I who am here, his Messenger, to-night,
But bring that presence to a point in light.
We are the agencies, the living laws,
Whereby Creation is eternal Cause.

" *This human life is no mere looking-glass,*
In which God sees His shadows as ye pass.
He did not start the pendulum of Time,
To go by Law, with one great swing sublime;
Resting Himself in lonely joy apart:
But to each pulse of life is beating heart.
And, as a Father sensitive, is stirred
By falling sparrow, or heart-wingèd word.

" *As the Babe's life within the Parent's, dim*
And deaf, ye dwell in God, a-dream of Him.
Ye stir and put forth feelers which are claspt
By airy hands and higher life is graspt.
As yet but darkly.   Life is in the root
And looking heavenward, from the ladder-foot,
Wingless as worms, with earthiness fast bound,
Up which ye mount but slowly, round on round.
Long climbing brings ye to the Father's knee;
Ye open gladsome eyes at last to see
That face of Love ye felt so inwardly.

" *In this vast universe of worlds no waif*
Of spirit looks to him but floateth safe.

No prayer so lowly but is heard on high;
And if a soul should sigh, and lift an eye,
He keeps that soul from sinking with a sigh.

" All life, down to the worm beneath the sod,
Hath spiritual relationships to God—
The Life of Life, the love of all, in all;
Lord of the large and infinitely small.

" Birds find their home across the pathless sea
By no hereditary memory.
From land to land they move, their way illumed
By the inflowing Love that bore them, plumed
For flight, thro' which the Mother Bird is taught
To   know   which   youngling   had   the   last   worm
      brought ;
The Insect led to garner food in nook
For young, on which it never lives to look.

" The veriest atoms, even as worlds above,
Are bridal chambers of creative Love,
Quick with the motion that suspends the whole
Of Matter spiral-spinning toward Soul.
And nothing is, but groping turns to Him,
Like babe to bosom, tho' the sight be dim :

Nothing but what reflects in some faint wise
The image that is God in Angel eyes—
The Infinite One, whose likeness we but see
Glassed in the Infinite of Variety :
Just as the waters fix a fluttering beam,
Caught in this chamber, and, with golden gleam,
Throw on the ceiling, limned in little, one
Pale image of the glory of the Sun !

" No seed of life blown down a dark abysm
Of earth or sea but feels the magnetism
That draws us Godward ! Flowers sunk in mines,
Or plants in ocean, where no sunbeam shines,
Will blindly climb up toward THEIR Deity,
Far off in Heaven, whom they can never see.

" There is a Spirit of Life within the Tree
That's fed and clothed from Heaven continually,
And does not draw all nourishment from earth.
It puts a myriad tender feelers forth,
That breathe in heaven and turn the breath to sap :
In every leaf it spreads a tiny lap
To take its manna from the hand of God
And gather force for fingers 'neath the sod

To clutch the earth with , moulds, from sun and rain,
Its leaves ; with spirit-life feeds every vein,
And thro' each vein makes wood for bough and bark :
Girth for the bole and rootage down the dark.

" So Man is fed by God and lives in Him :
Not merely nourished by his rootage dim
In a far Past ; a dead world underground,
But spirit to spirit reaches Heaven all round.

" Creative heat is current in the soul
From ages past, like sunshine in the coal,
Some fire of heaven in fossil stored away,
But spirit-life yet kindles at the ray
Warm from our Sun that shines in heaven to-day !

" Not in one primal Man before the Fall
Did God set life a-breathing once for all.
He is the breath of life from first to last ;
He liveth in the Present as the Past.
But ye, like rowers, turn your eyes behind ;
Ye look Without and vainly feel to find
Raised in relief, like letters for the blind,
The substance of that Glory in the mind.

" *Hints of the higher life, the better day,*
Visit the human soul, outlining aye
The perfect statue now rough-cast in clay;
And with a mournful sigh ye think and say
'This is the type that was, and passed away!'
God holds a flower to you, it only yields
The fragrance fading from forgotten fields.
'Ah, only Eden could have wafted it!'
Immortal imagery His hand hath writ
Within ye is with revelation lit
By secret shinings of the Infinite.
'These are but glimmers of a glory gone!'
I tell you they are prophecies of dawn
And glimpses of a life that still goes on.
Man hath not fall'n from Heaven, nor been cast
Out from some Golden Age lived in the Past!
His fall is from the possible Life before him:
His fall is from the Crown of Life held o'er
him.
Ye stoop by Corpse-light, groping on the ground,
And lo! the living God, a-shine all round!
Even while I speak there is a quickening,
The unrest of a world that feels the spring;
The crust o' the Letter cracks; new life takes wing;

A strong ground-swell will heave, a wave will break,
The Eternal grows more visibly awake.

" Upon the verge of sunrise ye but stand—
The door of life just open in your hand.
Behind you is the slip of space ye passed ;
Before you an illimitable vast.
Not backward point the footprints that ye trace
Of those who ran the foremost in the race,
With light of God full-shining on their face !
Look up, as Children of the Light, and see
That ye are bound FOR immortality,
Not passing FROM it : Heirs of Heaven ye,
Not Exiles.   God reverses human growth
For spirits ; they go ripening toward youth
For ever.   The fair Garden that still gleams
Across the desert, miraged in your dreams,
Smiles from the spirit, rather than the sod,
Wherever hallowed feet of Love have trod ;
Wherever souls yet walk and talk with God.
And Heaven is as near Earth now as when
The Angels visibly conversed with Men.
The Holy Dove that came to brighten down
Over the head of Christ, a heaven-dropt crown,

Now broods within ; it is the bosom-dove,—
It croons the music in the voice of Love.
'Neath human roofs still stoopeth the Divine
Closer than ever ; makes the heart its shrine.

" God hath been gradually forming Man
In His own image since the world began,
And is for ever working on the soul,
Like Sculptor on his Statue, till the whole
Expression of the upward life be wrought
Into some semblance of the Eternal Thought.
Race after Race hath caught its likeness of
The Maker as the eyes grew large with love.
But in one face alone ye look to see
The possible image smiling perfectly.

" Christ's was a conscious Birthday of the Soul.
Thenceforth the world on a broader gauge could
*   roll*
Out of old ruts : Man glimpse his glorious goal,
And leave the desert by-ways, darkly trod,
Heart-haunted by some gory ghost of God,
And Faith, exulting on its heavenward way,
Feel every dark should end at last in day.

No more vain searchings thro' the starry dome,
With vague blind yearnings for one hint of Home !
In Him ye see the Type Man climbs up to ;
The Model God is working from thro' you !
In Him ye have the nearest likeness given
On Earth of that hid face which is in heaven.

" You ask me ' how the lamp of life burns on
When all that visibly fed the flame is gone ?'

" Man does not live alone by visible breath,
And He who brings to life will lead thro' death.
Wait yet a little while and ye shall see
The flame was breathed on ; fed invisibly :
And that its motion springs with force seven-fold
When the life-heat is clasht against Death's cold.

" You think of spirit as prison-walled about
By substance, wondering how it can get out !
But to my vision radiates the soul
Thro' body ; by its pulses lights the whole
With life, and makes it luminous as the glass
Thro' which you see but only in spirit pass.
The wee babe nestled in the Mother's lap,
Feels her soul radiate in love and wrap

It softly in the very heart of bliss,
And draw all heaven thro' it in a kiss.

" As chalk is formed at bottom of the sea
From life that sheds its shell continually;
As bones are built up out of life's decay,
The body is shaped of substance sloughed away
From soul in ripening : 'tis a husk which yields
The earthy scaffold whereby spirit builds
Its heavenly house, that stands when the world-
    crust
Is made of dropt and perisht human dust.
Spirit is Lord and Master at the death,
As in beginning, of its house of breath.

" Man does not live alone by hunger and drouth,
But by the breath which kindles from God's
    mouth :
'Tis breathing spirit makes the body breathe,
And sets in outer type the life beneath.
So print makes visible the unseen thought
To pass away, the miracle being wrought.
Life is an inner energy, unfurled
In visible shows from an invisible world;

Still fed and fed from that almighty force
Of which no science yet hath grasped the source,
Whose infant germ from the dead seed reborn,
Is greater than a realm of ripened corn.
Like worlds warmed into being by their Sun,
Ye are embodied by the rays that run
Mysteriously across a gulf of night;
A bridge of spirit laid in beams of light.
And that which is the centre of the blaze
Travels in life unseen along the rays.
The book will pass; the living Mind work on;
The Visible fades; still shines the Eternal sun.

" I tell you these things are: I may not show
You how: there's much the senses cannot know.
Who knows the links of that invisible chain
Which runs from soul to soul, from brain to
        brain,
Whereby thought passes into other thought,
And out of sound its silent shape is wrought?
You see the miracle done before your eyes,
And in the flash of spirit to spirit dies
The common daylight: visual sense is blind
To see how Matter is made quick by Mind.

And there's a power in the hidden soul
To pass in at the eyes and print its whole
Self, in a picture finished infinitely
Beyond the portrait that the eyes can see.
Eyes ne'er behold your own souls face to face :
Your real selves invisibly embrace.

" You know not how a prayer ascends to God.
You saw no ladder Angel-feet e'er trod
In answer; hear no door turn on the hinge
When heaven opens, or the hells impinge
Upon the soul with their suggestion dark.
The Devil tempts, but how you cannot mark .
The bridge is still invisible that doth span
Your known and unknown: reach from God to
        Man.

" With labours infinite your Science seeks
Footing on inaccessible cloud-peaks.
Yet, must the Climbers know that there are things
Only attainable at last with wings.
That skies will not be scaled howe'er they clasp
The solid rock; that heaven still mocks their
        grasp.

On these they may not speak the final word.
On these the great Hereafter must be heard.
At best Man doth but darkly draw his light :
Each step ye take, each secret wrest from Night,
Must furnish food for faith as well as sight.

" The more ye feel the chain whereby ye are spanned,
The more its missing links elude the hand.
So Saturn's perfect rings, when, closer seen,
Are broken with dark gaps of night between !
Nor can ye more than mark the Visible shine
And in the gloom accept the Hand Divine.

" Live fruitfully the life ye may possess
With rootage beyond reach of consciousness,
And wait till the Unseen in flower blows.

" To find what gems lie hidden where it grows
Ye must not pluck the plant up by the root.
Wait till its treasures hang in precious fruit.

" There is no pathway Man hath ever trod
By faith or seeking sight but ends in God.
Yet 'tis in vain ye look Without to find
The inner secrets of the Eternal Mind,

Or meet the King on His external Throne.
But when ye kneel at heart, and feel so lone,
Perchance behind the veil you get the grip
And spirit-sign of secret fellowship;
Silently as the gathering of a tear
The human want will bring the helper near:
The very weakness, that is utterest need
Of God, will draw Him down with strength indeed.

" Enough to know ye live because He lives!
And love, because in love Himself He gives!
The gift is ever held sufficient sign
There is a Giver!   And if it be Divine
And like the Heaven ye dream, but may not see,
Giver Divine and Heaven there must be.

" Lean nearer to the Heart that beats thro' night:
Its curtain of the dark your veil of light.
Peace Halcyon-like to perfect Faith is given,
And it can float on a reflected Heaven
Surely as Knowledge that doth rest at last
Isled on its ' ATOM' in the unfathomed vast
Life-ocean, heaving thro' the infinite,
From out whose dark the shows of being flit,

In flashes of the climbing wave's white crest :
Some few a moment luminous o'er the rest !"

The voice ceased : the form faded in the beam
Of dawn, that swam down like the gladsome
    gleam
Of heaven to him who struggles, nearly
    drowned,
And draws him lifeward from the gulf profound,
And melts to a gold mist the dim green round.

PART VII

WHO hath not marked how graciously the Dawn
   Comes smiling when some stormy night
      hath gone?
As Beauty lifts the heaven of her eyes
Full on you large with their serene surprise
That you should dream such gentleness could dart
The looks that hurt you to the very heart!
Calm eyes, that thro' luxurious reaches roll
The richness of their rest on the vext soul.

So comes the Morning; new heavens rise above,
And open wider arms of larger love
Than ever: glad blue Ether, with the bliss
Of sunshine, laughs and kindles at its kiss.
There lie the tears of tempest, softly-bright
As Heaven had only rained in drops of light.
The air, an overflow of Heaven's own balm,
Nought but Earth's music breaks the divine calm.

H

Yet that same Morning looks on ruin and wreck,
And soothes a sea that lifeless swept the deck
Of some proud ship, and glorifies the wave
That landward heaves the mariner's glassy grave ;
Playfully rippling, shoaling goldenly o'er
Dead seamen dimly drifting to the shore !
Terribly innocent, Morning laughs on high,
While Ocean rocks them with its lullaby.

So came the Morning, smiling, crown'd with
    calm,
After my night of trouble, breathing balm.
Fair Earth with all her night-long-tearful eyes
A-sparkle with the soul of the sunrise !
On every blade there hung a drop of dew,
And every drop a live star shimmered thro' :
All phantoms of the night by shadowy stealth
Retired with Darkness from our world of health ;
All life unshrouded, to Heaven's influence bare,
Took wings of morning in the open air.
Our world, a warm safe nest of happy souls,
Basked in the brightness as the lily lolls
Her bosomed softness on the sunny stream,
Whose ripples lip her where she lies a-dream.

The stream, that crept a river of death by night,
Full of dark secrets, ran a river of light !
Such sense of rest to all glad things was given,
As earth were cradle of the peace of heaven.
A more than common freshness fed the breath
Of sweet new life ; there was no taint of death.
My nightmare over, I would dream no more
Of murder and the charnel at life's core ;
Or nameless creatures that may haunt old
    graves
Bat-like, and flit from out lone, twilight caves.

Green earth, glad heaven, gaily vied to win
Thought out-of-doors, yet would it brood within.
Sullen and shy as fish that will not rise
To any tempting lure of feathered flies,
But haunt the pool where, horribly quiet, lies
A dead child, with its wide-awake blue eyes.

Lonely I wandered in my garden-ground,
Musing on Life, the Death's-head rosily crown'd,
And of the mystery that clouds us round,
And of the mournful possibility
That, in some blindness, we may lose the key

Which to the keeping of each soul is given
To ope the door, and so be shut from Heaven;
Raking the ashes and the dust of death,
Long after we have done with human breath;
And of the features printed on my brain
In vision that would evermore remain,
And, any instant, sinister and swart
From out the light, at turn of eye, might start;
And I should see him! as 'neath the Tunnel's arc,
Where, down the shaft, day lightens thro' the dark,
Some chosen victim momently may mark
His murderer, with those snaky eyes at work
Fixed on him; in whose spark maglignant lurk
Cold fires of death drawn inward for the spring;
The dagger flash leaps in their glittering!

So, till its horrors almost lived to sight,
My spirit brooded o'er the bygone night;
Reflecting all the strife in upper air,
As you have seen, by some sea-margin, where
The circling sea-bird hovers, dreamily slow,
In likeness of the wave that sways below,
The Spirit of its motion on the wing:
Over that night my mind kept hovering.

At length the growing image of my thought
To some such final shape as this was wrought—

From end to end of things we may not see,
Nor square the circle of Eternity;
But, I can not believe in endless hell
And heaven side by side.   How could I dwell
Among the Saved, for thinking of the Lost?
With such a lot the Blest would suffer most.
Sitting at feast all in a Golden Home,
That towered over dungeon-grates of Doom,
My heart would ache for all the lost that go
To wail and weep in everlasting woe:
Thro' all the music I must hear the moan,
Too sharp for all the harps of Heaven to drown.

I cannot think of Life apart from Him
Who is the life, from cell to Seraphim:
And, if Hell flame unquenchably, must be
The life of hell to all eternity!
A God of love must expiate the stain
Of Sin Himself, by suffering endless pain;
Sit with eternal desolation round
His feet; his head with happy heavens crowned.

From Him the strength immortal must be sent,
By which the soul could bear the punishment.
I cannot think He gave us power to wring
From one brief life eternal suffering :
If this were so the Heavens must surely weep,
Till Hell were drown'd in one salt vast, sea-deep.
Forgive me, Lord, if wrongly I divine ;
I dare not think Thy pity less than mine.

I cannot image Heaven as Triumph-Car,
That rolleth red and reeking from the war,
Upborne on wheels of torture whirling round
With writhing souls for ever broke and bound !

God save me from that Heaven of the Elect,
Who half rejoice to count the numbers wreckt.
Because, such full weight to the balance given,
Sends up the scale that lands them surely in heaven.
And the proud Saved, exulting, soar the higher,
The lower that the Lost sink in hell-fire.

I think Heaven will not shut for evermore,
Without a knocker left upon the door,

Lest some belated Wanderer should come
Heart-broken, asking just to die at home,
So that the Father will at last forgive,
And looking on His face that soul shall live.
I think there will be Watchmen thro' the night,
Lest any, afar off, turn them to the light;
That He who loved us into life must be
A Father infinitely Fatherly,
And, groping for Him, these shall find their way
From outer dark, thro' twilight, into day.

I could not joy for Harvest gathered in,
If any souls, like tares and twitch of sin,
Were flung out by the Farmer to the fire,
Whose smoke of torment, rising high and higher,
Should fill the universe for evermore,
While we with glad feet trod the crystal floor
Thro' which the damned lookt up at Paradise,
For ever fixed, like fishes frozen in ice.

I could not sing the song of Harvest Home,
Thinking of those poor souls that never come;
Such mournful eyes from out their night would gleam
And haunt for ever all my happy dream!

Such tears,—lost jewels that flash God-ward, in
The dark, down-trodden Toad-like head of sin !

The New World's poorest emigrant will lend
A kindly hand to help a poorer friend.
And I must pray to God from out my bliss
For those who were beyond all help but His-—
Pray and repray, the same old prayer anew ;
Forgive them, Lord, they know not what they do.
Because they were so utterly accurst,
Self-doomed, that bitterness would be the worst.
O look down on them, from Thy place above,
The look of pity, Lord, half-way to love !

Mere human love, in this, its narrow sphere,
Can never think of those it once held dear,
Who, down the darkened way will pull apart,
But with a pitying eye ; an aching heart.
And still, as less the beckoning hand they heed,
The strength of Love grows with their greater need ;
The less they heed, the more it yearns to save.
And shall this love be dwarfed beyond the grave,
To lose, on wings, its feet-attainëd height ?
Better its blindness, than the eye of light

That coldly down on endless hell could glance,
With all its mortal sympathies in trance.

Or will some Lethean wave the soul caress,
And numb it into dull forgetfulness ;
Washing away all memory of distress
That others feel, while we but lift the hand
To pluck and eat the lotus of the land,
And those far wailings of the world of tears
Come mellowed into music for our ears,
With just the zestful dash of discord given,
That makes the pleasure pungent—perfects Heaven?

'Tis hard to read the Handwriting Divine ;
The vanishing *up-stroke* so invisibly fine !
There must be issues that we do not see.
The whole horizon of Futurity
Is nowise visible from where we stand ;
We are but dwellers in a lowly land.
We think the sun doth set, the sun doth rise,
And yet our world's but turning in the skies.
Seen from our lower level there must pass
Mysteries, so high and starry, we but glass

Them darkly, as we strain our mortal sight,
While 'twixt our souls and them there stands the
    night.
And then we scratch upon our window-pane,
Dimming its clearness, and we are so fain
To read our own imaginations fond,
For the true figures of the world beyond.
We model from the human life, and so
Feature the future from the face we know.
'Tis always sunless one side of our globe,
And thus we fashion the Eternal's robe !
God made Man in His image, but our plan's
To mould and make God's image in the Man's,
And if my thought be human as the rest,
At least the likeness shall be Man's at best.
Too long hath Calvin's spectrum sacrificed,
Smoke-hued with hell, the pure white light of Christ !

Our Science grasps with its transforming hand ;
Makes real, half the tales of wonder-land.
We turn the deathliest fetor to perfume ;
We give decay new life and rosy bloom ;
Change filthy rags to paper virgin white ;
Make pure in spirit what was foul to sight.

Even dead, recoiling force, to a fairy gift
Of help is turned, and taught to deftly lift.
How can we think God hath no crucible
Save that Black Country of a burning Hell?
Or the great ocean of Almighty power,
No scope to take the life-stream from our shore,
Muddy and dark, and make it pure once more?

Dear God, it seems to me that Love must be
The Missionary of Eternity!
Must still find work, in worlds beyond the grave,
So long as there's a single soul to save;
Must, from the highest heaven, yearn to tell
Thy message; be the Christ to some dark hell;
That all divergent lines at length will meet
To make the clasping round of Love complete;
The rift 'twixt Sense and Spirit will be healed,
Ere the Redeemer's work be crowned and sealed;
Evil shall die like dung about the root
Of Good, or climb converted into fruit!
The discords cease, and all their strife shall be
Resolved in one vast peaceful harmony:
That all these accidents of Time and breath
Shall bear no black seal of a Second Death:

That, freed from branding heats that burn in Time,
The lost *Black Race* shall whiten in that clime :
All blots of error bleacht in Heaven's sight ;
All life's perplexing colours lost in light :
That Thou hast power to work out every stain,
That purifying is the end of Pain ;
And, waking, we shall know what we but dream
Dimly, that punishment is to redeem ;
And here, or There, the penitent thrill must
　　　leaven
The earthiest soul and wing it toward Heaven ;
That when the Angel-Reapers shall up-sheave
The harvest, Angel-Gleaners will not leave
One least small grain of good—and there are
　　　none
So evil but some precious germ lives on,—
The grimiest gutter crawling by the way
Still hath its reflex of the face of Day ;—
And all the seeds divine foredoomed by fate
To bear blind blossoms here shall germinate
And have another chance, in other place,
Where tears of gratitude and dews of grace
Shall warm and quicken to the feeblest root,
Till in Thy garden they are ripe for fruit.

So shall we find the Dark of our old Earth
Twin with the eternal Daylight from the birth,
And trodden in the grave-dust we shall see
This serpent-symbol of Eternity
That only maketh ends meet, head and tail,
A world all blessing with a world all bale.

Thus, in its maze, my mind went round and round,—
Like him, lost in the Bush, who thought he found
The pathway that he sought, because he beat
His track with constant tread of his own feet,—
As round the dew-drencht garden-walks I went
Till, pausing, all unconscious of intent,
Nigh where a greenery of Syringas grew
And, shedding shadow round, there leaned a Yew,—
Sombrely ancient watcher by the tomb !
A Nest of Thrushes the live heart o' the gloom ;
I saw the earth was crackt, where recent rain
Had crusht and crumbled in a new-made drain,
And human bones were plainly peering thro',
As if Death grinned and show'd a tooth or two !
I searcht, and, ere the ghastly work was done,
Had gathered half a tiny skeleton,
That had been once a Child.

                              And then it came
On me that in my dream I saw the same,
And had been warned to calcine them in flame,
And pound them small as is the finest rust,
And on the winds of heaven fling the dust.
I did it, and, altho' that soul accurst
Still walks the darkness, we had passed the worst,
And there was peace o' nights at the Haunted
    Hurst.

IN MEMORIAM.

THIS record of affectionate remembrance, inscribed to the Lady Marian Alford on the death of her son, John William Spencer, Earl Brownlow, as the Author's offering of sympathy in the common sorrow, has, in an earlier shape, together with other memorial poems, already appeared in *Good Words*, and thus had the advantage of being held out as it were at arm's length to be retouched.

The dear ones who are worthiest of our love
Below, are also worthiest above.
Too lofty is his place in glory now,
For hands like ours to reach and wreathe his brow :
A few poor flowers we plant upon his tomb,
Watered with tears to make them breathe and bloom.
The gentle soul that was so long thy ward,
Now hovers over thee, thine Angel-Guard :
And, as thou mourn'st above his dust so dear,
Thy happy Comforter draws smiling near.
  Look up, dear friend, our Doves of Earth but rise,
  Transfigured into Birds of Paradise.

" The idea of his life doth sweetly creep
Into my study of imagination ;
And every lovely organ of his life
Will come apparelled in more precious habit—
More moving delicate, and full of life,
Into the eye and prospect of my soul
Than when he lived indeed."

APPARELLED richly in presence of the Gods,
 With crown upon his brow, the old Greek
  stood
And offered up his soul at Sacrifice.
Even then the tidings came,—"THY SON IS DEAD."

 .

They saw the sharp words pierce him through
 and through,
The firm lip quiver and the face grow white;
They saw the strong man tremble to the knees:
Slowly the big drops gathered in his eyes:
Slowly he took the crown from off his head,
And let it fall to the ground, as one who feels
Heart-broke all over,—for his pride of life
Hath faded, and his strength is spilled in dust.

But, when the Messenger went on to tell
The exulting story—how the valiant youth
Had lost a life to win a Country's love ;
How bravely he had borne him in the battle ;
How well he fought, how gloriously he fell ;
The weeping Father put his war-look on
And rose up with the stature of his soul—
All his life listening at the hungry ear—
Eyes burning with the splendour of quenched
          tears—
His pillared chin firm-set, his brave mouth clenched
In calm resolve to bear, and on his face
A smile as if of Sword-light !
                              Then he stooped,
And gently took the crown up from the ground ;   ·
Softly replaced it on his brow, and wore
It proudly, as the visible symbol of
That other awful crown which darkened down.

So, when the word came that our friend was dead,
We bowed beneath the burden of our loss,
And could have grovelled straightway, prone in
          dust.
But looking on the happy death he died,

And thinking of the holy life he lived,
And knowing he was one of those that soon
Attain their starry stature, and are crown'd,
We could not linger in the dust to weep,
But were upborne from earth as if on wings;
A sunbeam in the soul dried up the tears,
In which the sorrow trembled to be gone;
For his dear sake we could afford to smile.

Why should we weep, when 'tis so well with him?
Our loss even cannot measure his great gain!
Why should we weep when death is but a mask
Thro' which we know the face of Life beyond?
Grief did but bow us at his grave to show
Far more of Heaven in the landscape round!

For such a vestal soul as his,—so pure,
So crystal-clear, so filled with light, we lookt
As at some window of the other world,
And almost saw the Angel smiling through—
'Twas but a step from out our muddy street
Of Earth, on to the pavement all of pearl!

Why should we weep? We do not bury love;
We cannot seek that jewel in the grave!

The dust of earth but claims its kindred dust :
We do not bury life, and cannot feel
The grave-grass grow betwixt our warmth and
    him ;
Death emptieth the House but not the Heart :
That keeps its darlings safe tho' out of sight.

Let us uplift the eyelids of the Mind
And see the living Love who dwelt awhile
In that frail body, now a spirit of Light
All jubilant upon the hills of God.
This gloom we feel, this mourning that we wear,
Is but the Shadow of his lordlier height.

Why should they weep who have another friend
In death ; another thread to guide them thro'
Life's maze ; another tie to draw them home ;
A firmer foothold in the infinite ;
Another kinsman on the spiritual side ;
Another voice to greet them thro' the Void ;
Another face to kindle with its life
The pale impersonality of God ?

The dearest souls, you know, must part in sleep,
And death is but a little longer night.

A little while, and we shall wake to find
Our lost ones with us face to face, and feel
All years of yearning summed up in a kiss.

Why should we fear the Grave? It is the bed
Where the King lay in State with Angels round,
And hallowed it for evermore to us.
Why should we fear the Grave? It is the way
The Conqueror went, and made the very dust
Grow starry with the sparkle of his splendour,
And left the darkness conscious of His presence.
We can look down upon the Grave now He
Has plumbed it, spanned it, one foot on each side.

Thro' His dear love who hath abolished death,
We may shut up our Graveyards of the heart
That lookt so grim of old, and plant anew
This garden of our God to smile with flowers.

Why do we shrink so from Eternity?
We are in Eternity from Birth not Death!
Eternity is not beyond the stars—
Some far Hereafter—it is *Here*, and *Now* !

The Kingdom of Heaven is *within*, so near
We do not see it save by spirit-sight.
We shut our eyes in prayer, and we are *There*
In thought, and Thoughts are spirit-*things*—
Realities upon the other side.
In death we close our eyelids once for all
To pass for ever, and seem far away.
And yet the distance does not lie in death :
Death's not the only door of spirit-world,
Nor Visibility sole presence-sign :
The Near or Far is in our depth of love
And height of life : We look WITHOUT, to find
Our lost ones are beyond all human reach :
We feel *Within*, and lo ! they are nestling near.

Flow soft, ye tears, adown my Lady's face,
And bathe the broken spirit with your balm,
And melt the cloud about her into drops
That glister with the light of Heaven's own smile.
And thou, God, whisper as the tears do fall,
No cloud would rise to rain but for Thy Sun !
She sorroweth not as those who have no hope,
Nor is her House left wholly desolate.
O Grief, lie lightly on my Lady's brow :

She gave her best of life in love for him !
A crown of glory wears the dear bowed head
That hath grown grey in noble sacrifice.

Ah me, I know the heart must have its way.
I know the ache of utter loneliness ;
The distance between those that were so near ;
The silence never broken by a sound
We still keep listening for ; the spirit's loss
Of its old clinging-place, that makes our life
A dead leaf drifting desolately free :
The many thousand things we had to say ;
And on the dear still face that hushing look,
As though the sweet life-music still went on
Though too far off for hearing—(as it doth) !
Thrice have I wrestled and been thrown by Death,
Thrice have I given my dear ones to the grave ;
And yet I know—see it in spite of tears :
Say it, even while the heart breaks in the voice :
These are His ways to draw us nearer Him.
And we must climb by pathways of the cloud.

He breaks the image to reveal Himself!
He takes our dearest things to woo us with ;

Takes, for a little while, the gift He gave
For ever: but to better still our best.

Feeling for that which fled, our finite love
Is caught up in the clasp o' the Infinite,
Palpably as tho' God did press the hand
And make the heart well up and flood the eyes
With that proud overflow of a fuller Heaven!

O Lady, let mine be the songbird's part,
That singeth after rain and shakes the drops
Down, with his thrillings, from the drooping spray,
And sets it softly springing nigher Heaven
That smiles out 'twixt the clouds with gladdest
          blue!
Your love-ties have but lengthened to let free
The shadowed soul that needed far more sun.
So the fair Lily,* growing down the dark
Beside her lover, yearneth towards Heaven
And lives up faster, till she springs afloat,
To sun her on the surface of the stream:

---

* The " *Vallisneria*," the male and female flowers of which appear
on separate plants; the latter blooming on the surface of the water,
while the former tears its roots from the soil to rise and blossom and
die beside it.

And now she draws up, even by the root,
Her Love left pining on the earth below,
Lifting him to her side again, full flower;
And 'tis his Heaven to die and get to her!

What did we ask, with all our love for him,
But just a little breath of fuller life,
To float the labouring lungs? And God hath given
Him Life itself; full, everlasting Life!
What did we pray for? Rest, even for a night,
That he might rise with Sleep's most golden dews
Refreshed, to feel the morning in his soul?
And God hath given him His Eternal Rest.
We could not offer freedom for one hour
From that dread weight of weariness they bear
Who try for years to shake Death's Shadow off:
And God hath made him free for Evermore.

Before me hangs his Picture on the wall,
Alive still, with the loving, cordial eyes.—
How tenderly their winsome lustre laughed!—
The fine pale face, pathetically sweet,
So thin with suffering that it seemed a soul:
We feared the Angels might be kissing it

Too often, and too wooingly for us :
The hands, so delicate and woman-white,
That day by day were gliding from our grasp :
They used to make my heart ache many a time.

I see another picture now. The form
Ye sowed in weakness hath been raised in power ;
A palace of pleasure for a prison of pain.
The beauty of his nature that we felt
Is featured in the shape he weareth now !
The same kind face, but changed and glorified ;
From Life's unclouded summit it looks back,
And sweetly smiles at all the sorrows past,
With such a look as taketh away grief :
No longer pale, and there is no more pain.
His face is rosed with Heaven's immortal bloom,
For he hath found the land of Health at last ;
The One Physician who can cure all ills :
And he hath eaten of the Tree of Life,
And felt the Eternal Spring in brain and breast
Make lusty life that lightens forth in love.

Indeed, indeed, as the old Poet saith,
He was a very perfect, gentle Knight !

A natural Noble, by the grace of God :
Affection in the dearest human form.
Yet, gentle as he was, how gallantly
He bore his sufferings, kept the worst from sight,
Having the heroic flash of English blood.
How freely would he spend his little hoard
Of saved-up strength with spirit lordly and blithe,
To enrich a welcome and make gladder cheer !

And to the Poor he was all tender heart.
The very last time that he talked with me
His trouble was to know how poor folks lived
Upon so small a pittance, and he sighed
For life, for strength to do more than he could,
And in his kingly eyes great sorrow reigned.

No sighs, no weakness now, in that glad world
Where yearning avails more than working here,
And to desire is to accomplish good :
For Wishes get them wings of power, and range
Rejoicing thro' illimitable life ;
And we shall find some Castles built in Air
Stand good ; are habitable after all !

To me, his life is like the innocent Flower
That springs up for the light and spreads for love;
Breathes fragrantly in gratitude to God,
And in sweet odours passes from our sight.
But there's no jot of all his promise lost :—
Each golden hint shall have fulfilment yet—
All that was heavenliest perfected in heaven.

All the shy modesties of secret soul
That breathed like violets hidden in the dusk;
The folded sweetness, the unfingered bloom;
The unsunned riches of his rarer self;
Are shut up softly to be saved by Him
Who gave us of the Flower, but keeps the fruit.

The best his life could grow on earth is given;
The rest can ripen till ye meet in heaven.

And dear my Lady, little can we guess
What God hath planned for those He loves so
      much,
And beckons home so early to Himself!
May some full foretaste of his perfect peace
Fall on you, solacing with solemn joy.

Of such as he was, there be few on Earth,
Of such as he is, there are many in Heaven;
And Life is all the sweeter that he lived,
And all he loved more sacred for his sake:
And Death is all the brighter that he died,
And Heaven is all the happier that he's there.

So, one by one the dear old faces fade.
Hands wave their far farewell while beckoning us
Across the river, all must pass alone.
We stand at gaze upon their shining track,
Until the two worlds mingle in a mist,
And the two lives are molten into one:
Familiar things grow phantom-like remote;
Things visionary draw familiar-near;
The picture that we gaze on seems the Real
Looking at us, and we the Shadows that pass.

And yet 'tis sweet to feel—as underfoot,
OUR path slopes for the quiet place apart;
Day darkens in the Valley of Death's shade—
Our best half landed in the better life;
The balance leaning to the other side;
The peaceful evening comes that brings all home,

And we are weaning kindly to leave go
Our hold of earth; life in the Autumn-leaf
Loosens with every shower; and as the gloom
Gathers, and things are growing all a-dusk,
We know our Stars are smiling overhead,
In their eternal setting high and safe
Where they can look down on our passing night,
Glad in the loftier radiance of a sun
We may not see, with steadfast gaze of love
Unfathomable as Eternity:
Dear memories of Vesper gentleness
That are the Phosphor hopes of coming day,
And death grows radiant with our Shining Ones.

Blessëd are they whose treasures are in Heaven!
Their grief's too rich for our poor comforting.
Let us put on the robe of readiness,
The golden trumpet will be sounding soon,
That bids us to the gathering in the Heavens!
Let us press forward to their summit of life
Who have ceased to pant for breath and won their
        Rest,
And there is no more parting, no more pain!

CARMINA NUPTIALIA.

The Story of all stories, sweet and old ;
Sweetest to Lovers the last time 'tis told.

CARMINA NUPTIALIA.

WEDDED LOVE.

THIS little spring of life, that feeds the root
    Of England's greatness, giveth, underground,
Bloom to the Flower, and freshness to the Fruit ;
    Then wells and spreads, with golden ripples
        round,
In circling glory to a sea of might,
    Embracing Home and Country of our love :
Half-mirroring the beauty beyond sight—
    Taking some likeness of the abode above.

K

THE WEDDING.

ALL Women love a Wedding ! old
    Or youthful ; Mother, Widow, or Wife :
It lights with precious gleam of gold
    The river of poorest life :

For one, the gold is far and dim ;
    For one, a glimpse of things to be ;
But here it sparkles, at the brim
    Of full felicity !

And they will cluster by the way ;
    Crowd at this Eden-gate, with eyes
That run, and pray that this Pair may
    Keep their new Paradise.

Green is the garden, as at first ;
    As smiling-blue the happy skies,
Where float the bubble-worlds that burst,
      And leave us smarting eyes.

They seem to think that these *must* clasp
    The jewel turned to dew or mist :
The glamour they could never grasp,
      Tho' wedded lips have kissed ;

That this gold Apple of promise, crown'd
    With redness on the sunny side,
Will gradually grow ripe all round ;
      That this new Lover and Bride

Must reach the breathing Magic Rose
    Such cunning spirits hold in air,
On which our fingers could not close,
      Even when we knew 'twas there !

This nest of hopes will bring forth young
    Unto the brooding heart's low call—
Not merely pretty birds'-eggs, strung
      To hide a naked wall !

So many start thus, hand-in-hand—
   Few only reach the blessed goal;
But *these* shall surely see the land
     Hid somewhere in the soul.

And delicate airs creep sweetly through
   Old bridal-chambers dusty and dim:
Down from a far heaven warm and blue,
     The mellow splendours swim.

The Woman's eyes grow loving wet;
   They dazzle with the morning ray:
The Woman's longing will beget
     Her own dear wedding-day!

In his network of wrinkles, Age
   May veil their virgin beauties now;
Faces be furrowed—a strange page
     Of writing on the brow:

The smiling soul cannot erase
   The sad life-lines it shines above;
Yet, imaged in the dear old face,
     You see their own young love!

The sleeping Beauty wakes anew
 Beneath the touch of tender tears ;
The Flower unfolds, to drink the dew,
  That seemëd dead for years.

All hearts are as a grove of birds
 Spring-toucht and chirruping every one ;
And each will set the Wedding-Words
  To a music of her own.

Some withered remnant of old bliss
 Flushing on faded cheeks they bring,
Telling of times when Love's young kiss
  Was a fire-offering ;

And spirits walk in white, as starts
 This bridal-tint that blooms anew ;
And so, with all their Woman-hearts,
  They fling Good Luck's old shoe !

SERENADE.

" AWAKE, *sweet Love, for Heaven is awake,*
    And waiting to be gracious for thy sake!
All night I saw thy fairness gleam afar
With fresh, pure sparkle of the Morning-Star ·
Awake, my Love, and let the veil be drawn
From Beauty bathëd at the springs of Dawn.

" *Awake, sweet Love, for Heaven is awake,*
And waiting to be gracious for thy sake.
    A touch upon some silver-sounding string,
    As all the harps of heaven were vibrating
    Within me, woke me, bade me rise and say
    ' *Awake, my Love, this is our wedding-day.'*

" *Awake, sweet Love, for Heaven is awake,*
And waiting to be gracious for thy sake.
 It is the tender time when turtle-doves
 Begin to murmur of their vernal loves :
 Spirits that all night nestled in the flowers
 Shake perfume from their wings this hour of
  hours.

" *Awake, sweet Love, for Heaven is awake,*
And waiting to be gracious for thy sake.
 To feel thee mine my faith is large enough,
 And yet the miracle needs continual proof !
 One minute satisfied, the next I pine
 For just one more assurance thou art mine.

" *Awake, sweet Love, for Heaven is awake,*
And waiting to be gracious for thy sake.
 Thy presence sets my cloudland round about
 Glowing as heaven were turning inside out :
 And all the mists that darkened me erewhile
 Are smitten into splendours at thy smile.

" *Awake, sweet Love, for Heaven is awake,*
And waiting to be gracious for thy sake.

Our great sunrise of life begins to glow,
And all the buds of love are ripe to blow ;
And all the Birds of Bliss are gaily singing,
And all the Bridal-Bells of Heaven are ringing."

" WHEN *first my true Love crown'd me with her
   smile,*
Methought that heaven encircled me the while!
When first my true Love to mine arms was given,
Ah, then methought that I encircled Heaven."

AN APRIL WEDDING.

O APRIL Wedding,
   Sad-smiling, shadowy-bright ;
The Grave at foot, and overhead
   The merry Bird of Light !

O April Wedding,
   The conscious ear at times
Detects the Bell that tolled the knell
   Among the Marriage-Chimes !

O April Wedding,
   Thy hues together run,—
Thro' wet eyes seen.—as Red and Green
   Dazzle till they grow one !

O April Wedding,
　　Where Love is crown'd in tears,
And on a ground of deepest gloom,
　　Hope's brightest Bow appears !

O April Wedding,
　　In glittering sun and showers
The very grave looks glad To-day,
　　And dead hands offer flowers !

O April Wedding,
　　Thy clouds go all in white ;
Those that darkliest wept now smile
　　Most glorified in light !

LEAVE-TAKING.

WHEN the wings are feathered,
   The birds forsake their nest;
So the Bride will leave her Home
   Leaning to her Lover's breast.
The tear was in her eye,
   But the soul was smiling through,
Brimful of sunshine
   As a drop of summer dew.

AS THEY PASSED.

WITHIN Love's chariot, side by side,
    Sweetness and Strength did never ride
More perfectly personified :
    One of the dearest Angels out
    Of Heaven, the Bride was, beyond doubt ;
    And his a Manhood fit to be
    The mortal Mansion of some deity.
    All eyes, like jewels, on them hung
      Glowing with precious life,
    As at her Husband's side she clung
      The nestled, new-made Wife !
Glad were they in the happiness they gave,
But in their own proud pleasure they were grave.

IN the presence of Spring, *our* beautiful Spring,
    Blithe bird of the Bosom! the heart will sing.
A Spirit of Joy in the oldest breast
Is stirring, and making it young as the rest :
Wakes a new life to leap in each limb,
And laugh out of eyes that were wintry and dim ;
So the old Wine stirs in his winter gloom,
And wants to waken, and climb, and bloom,
As he used to do in the world outside,
When grapes grew big in their purple of pride.
He would laugh in the light, he would flush in the
    foam ;
In a care-drowning wave he would rosily roam ;
For his blood is so mellow, so merry, so warm,
Into spirit of joy it would fain transform,

And in human life keep holiday—
Rioting ruddily, ripple and play;
Break on the brain in a luminous spray,
Tinting with heaven our earthly clay;
In a fiery chariot mount on its way,
With spirit-company, lordly and gay,
And pass like a soul that is lost in day.
So the Spirit of Joy in the oldest breast
Is stirring, and making it young as the rest;
Wakes a new life to leap in each limb,
And laugh out of eyes that were wintry and dim.
Blithe bird of the bosom! the heart will sing
In the presence of Spring, *our* beautiful Spring.

A FACT THAT FLOWERS DOUBLE.

ENGLISH John Talbot, Shakspeare's terribly
      brave
Great Fighter, lay in his forgotten grave.
It was but yesterday they found his dust,
The sheath of that old Sword all gone to rust
In English earth ; his burial-place recover
In lands owned by a certain Lordly Lover.
And, lo ! a Rose had sprung from out his tomb,
And climbed about the Lover's life to bloom :
A peerless flower of the old Hero's stock—
The tenderest gush from that heroic rock.
Not oft doth Fate vouchsafe so plain a sign,
Prefiguring the lives that are to twine.
All sweetness to this wedded life be given ;
Its root so deep in earth, its perfect flower in
      heaven.

A WAYSIDE WHISPER.

" SEVEN years I served for you,
    To Love, our lord of life,
Ere he made me a Master
    And I won you for my wife,—
So faithfully, so fondly,
    Through a world of doubts and fears,
Seven long years, Belovëd !
    Seven long years.

" Seven years you beaconed me—
    My leading, crowning star,
To climb the Mount of Manhood,
    And you drew me from afar :

L

You made my grey hours golden,
  You glistened through my tears,
Seven long years, Belovëd !
  Seven long years.

" Sometimes you shined so near me—
  Far as we dwelt apart—
I hardly sought you with my arms
  You were so safe at heart !
Sometimes you dwined *so distant*
  I bowed with solemn fears ;
Seven long years, Belovëd !
  Seven long years.

" I built my Arch of Triumph
  For you to ride through ;
I kept my lamps all lighted
  That the warring winds outblew :
I worked and I waited
  And I fought down my fears,
Seven long years, Belovëd !
  Seven long years.

" Now the perils are all over,
  And the pains all past,

My fortune's wheel full-circle comes
  In your dear eyes at last!
For such a prize the winning
  Most brief and poor appears,
Yet, 'twas seven long years, Belovëd!
  Seven long years."

THE WELCOME HOME.

WARM is the Welcome! 'tis our way to grasp
  The hand in love or greeting till it ache ;
But to a tender heart our love doth take
The happy pair it doth so proudly clasp.

And very tender in its love To-day
  Is every heart toucht with a thought of Him
  Low-lying in the Cypress-shadow dim,
From which we came to waft you on your way,

And the still face, that looks from Ashridge towers
  With smile more regnant in its touching ruth,
  And sad hoar-frost upon the dews of youth,
And Widow's weeds to mix with bridal-flowers.

Through Him we lost, we have more love to give.
   As some fond Mother yearningly hath breathed
   Her life out in the new life she bequeathed,
Our dearest died that this great love might live.

These darling Violets, eloquently mute,
   Are rich in sadder bloom and sweeter breath,
   And that pathetic sanctity of death,
Because our buried joy was at their root.

These Roses blush with a more vital glow
   Of crimson—like pale buds, whose tips are red
   As tho' the flower's heart, in breaking, bled—
Because of looks so lately wan with woe.

These are our Jewels! tears that purged our sight
   Like Euphrasy; they lay above the Dead
   All drear and dim; but the sad drops we shed
Now live with twinkling lustres in Your light!

The love that darkly wept at heart hath risen
   Transfigured. See its sunburst in each face!
   As Earth, with all her flowers, smiles embrace
To Spring, rejoicing from her wintry prison.

These Voices, mounting merry as Larks up-spring,
    But now were praying on the low, cold sod :
    The night is past—they soar in praise to God ;
They make the old English greeting rarely ring.

We lean and look to You, thinking of Him.
    Warm welcome for the sake of One that's gone ;
    Warm welcome for your own ! Pass on, pass on ;
We wave our hands, and shout till sight grows dim :

And, ere the shouts cease ringing in your ears,
    We drink a health—all standing—drink to you,
    While in our eyes the tears are standing too :
Old tears, that wanted to be wept for years :

But keep a holy hush mid all the noise,
    To match the silent music your hearts make :
    Pass on into your faëry heaven, and take
Our gentlest blessing on your wedded joys.

The dawn *will* rise, tho' golden days be set ;
    The birds sing merrily, in spite of Death ;
    Young hearts will love while lasts this human
        breath ;
Rainbows bridge Earth and Heaven for eyes tear-wet.

Pass *gaily* on in glory through the gate
  Of your new life, beneath this Bridal-Dawn ;
  And when from future days the veil is drawn
All happy fortunes for you lie in wait !

And, looking on your bliss, with proudest flush
  May the dear Mother's face be glorified.
  We, now the sound hath ceased, will stand
    outside
Your Portals—all hearts praying mid the hush.

THE BONNY BRIDELAND FLOWER.

IN the Brideland sleeping,
  Nestled Beauty's Flower;
Came the Lover peeping
  Into her green bower;
On her face hung tender
  As a drop of dew;
With her virgin splendour
  Thrilling through and through.

Now, the shy, sweet maiden
  Softly droops her head:
All her heart is laden
  With his coming tread!

Now the new dawn breaketh
    In a blush of bliss ;
The Belovëd waketh
    At her Troth-love's kiss.

In our dull grey weather
    We have seen her bloom ;
Fain as Exiles gather
    Round some flower from Home ;
Seen the face that never
    Fades away, but gleams,
With its still smile, ever
    Through the land of Dreams.

Fair befall the bonny,
    Bonny Brideland flower !
All things dear and sunny
    Bless her bridal bower !
Truest love e'er given
    Feed her new life-root ;
And thou God in heaven,
    Crown the flower with fruit.

A LOVER'S SONG.

"ONE so fair—none so fair.
    In her eyes so true
Love's most inner Heaven bare
    To the balmiest blue!

" One so fair—none so fair.
    In the skies no Star
Like my Star of Earth so near—
    They but shine afar.

" One so fair—none so fair.
    All too sweet it seems :
Wake me not, O world of care,
    If I walk in dreams.

" *One so fair—none so fair.*
    O my bosom-guest,
Love ne'er smiled a happier pair
    To the bridal-nest.

" *One so fair—none so fair.*
    Lean to me, sweet Wife:
Light will be the load we bear:
    Two hearts in one life."

THE MARRIED LIFE.

O HAPPY love of weans and Wife,
　　Ye make a man's heart dance;
Kindle the desert face of life
　　With colours of romance:

A Land of Promise sparkles where
　　Your rosier light hath shone;
Too distant to attain, but near
　　Enough to tempt us on.

'Tis here that Heaven striketh root
　　To give the Immortal birth,
Man tastes the unforbidden fruit
　　That deifies on earth.

All ye that such a Garden own,
  Of wingèd thieves beware,
And trifles, light as thistle-down,
  That sow the seeds of care.

Only in singleness of heart,
  Ye keep the heaven ye win !
When Wife and Husband pull apart
  The Serpent will slide in.

VIA CRUCIS VIA LUCIS.

SPITE of the Mask Eternal Love doth wear
   At times, that makes us shrink from it in fear,
Because the Father's face we cannot find,
Nor feel the presence of His love behind,
Nature at heart is very pitiful.

How gentle is the hand doth kindly pull
The coverlet of flowers over the face
Of Death, and light up his dark dwelling-place !
With fingers and with foot-fall soft and low
She comes to make the quiet mosses grow :
Safe-smiling, draws the Snowdrop thro' the snow.
Busy in sun and rain, she strives to heal,
Doing her best to comfort or conceal :

With tenderest grass makes green the saddest
     grave,
And over death her flags of life *will* wave.
She is the Angel, waiting by the prison,
That saith, "*He is not here, he is arisen,*"
When lorn in soul we seek the face we knew,
And dream of buried sweetness coming through
The earth in spring-time, every flower a smile
Of that dear Presence we have lost awhile.

Thus, on our old Crimean battle-ground,
A poor, unknown, dead Soldier's bones were
     found—
(*Known* with those noble Englishmen of ours !)
When the next May came with her sweet Wild
     Flowers,
Nestled they lay above-ground in a grave
Of tall, plumed grass, funereally a-wave
In the West wind that breathed of Home : and
     tender
There rose from earth a dawn of such spring-splen-
     dour,
As if the heavens were breaking thro' the tomb :
The Wild Flowers had so buried them in bloom.

And, if we lift our eyes up from the ground,
We see how surely life is compassed round
With the Divine, that doth so kindly bound
The pitiless blaze of fires that soon would scorch
To ashes and put out our tiny torch
Of being; veil the vastness of the Whole,
As with droopt eyelids for the naked soul.

The silent Ministers of Healing crowd
About the broken heart and spirit bowed,
To stay the bleeding with immortal balm,
And still the cries with wings of blessèd calm;
Out of the old death make the new life spring,
Our earthly-buried hopes take homeward wing;
And to each blinding tear that dimmed our sight,
They give a starrier self; a Spirit of Light.

No matter in what separate lives we range,
We feel a rootage deeper than all change.
We know the roses flower to fade: We know
The roses also fade again to blow.
Death is Life's Shadow!

                    Mute the music looks,
And dark and dead when shadowed in the books:

Do but interpret it, all heaven will roll
The Life of Music thro' the echoing soul.

So we grow friends, familiar friends, with Death ;
Can look up in his face with firmer faith,
To see the frowning brows shade tender eyes,
Like sunny openings into Paradise.

Through all the gloom and stillness of distress,
With life all muffled up in silentness,
We voyage on — ice-locked, snow-blind, frost-
    bound—
Like Sailors with the Arctic winter round,
Who thought they stranded in the dark, and found
The solid water all one floating ground ;
And drifted through the night, divinely drawn,
Out to the open sea, where daylight shone.

The Shadow of Death is changed into the Dawn,
That radiant Angel of Eternity !
The mourners look up from the grave to see
The dark, that bowed them by its awfulness,
Fell from the Father's hands, spread out to
    bless.

M

So, in His own good season, God hath given
This beautiful Joy-Bringer from His Heaven,
To bear His benediction from above,
And be the smiling Presence of His love!

" *I go, but I will send the Comforter!*"
The gracious promise is fulfilled in Her.
Though heaviness endureth for a night,
Joy cometh with the morning.   Lo! the Light.
Gone is the winter from our spirit clime;
This is the herald of our golden time.
In all the beauty of promise, Spring is here—
Our Spring—that will be with us all the
     year.

O, beautiful Joy-Bringer! everywhere
Happiness smiles around you, like an air
Of glory, which you dwell in—Phosphor-fair!
The lives that have in mourning darkling lain
Now gather colour; sun them once again.
The tender shine that cometh after rain
Illumes the eyes of old heart-ache: the pain
Of loss transmuted to all-golden gain.

Just now we are in the shadow of coming change,
And faces darken, and old things grow strange ;
And from the new Unknown a many shrink.
Our world is getting tilted,* Sages think.
" *The wine of life is drawn, and the mere lees* "
All that is left us.   Shame on fears like these !
Whate'er Eclipse may come, storm-signals threat,
There's room for noble life in England yet.
As in the very heart of Hope we'll ride,
Borne on the ninth wave of our triumph's tide,
That with its new life heaves Old England's
        breast,
Only be loyal to the Loftiest ;
Arise and crown old sanctities anew,
By nobler conquest make your lordship true ;
Awake the spirit in our English blood,
That slowly brightens to the fervid flood,
And does not flash till the leap comes that shows
Power all the lustier for its long repose.
And if the proudest Nobles have to bow,
Then let it be as Rowers bend to row
A sturdier stroke ; and faint not, tho' we know
Not under what dark arch we have to go.

                    * Astronomically.

But win the nod of an approving soul,
Even tho' ye never reach your chosen goal.

O ! young hearts, dancing to the rise and fall
Of life's most winsome tune at festival,
Looking on your new world wherein ye move
With all the large, sweet wonder of young love,
The moments thronging with the life of years ;
Crowded with happiness and quick to tears ;
New smiles of greeting in each minute's face ;
New worlds of pleasure brimming every space ;
This is no winter-withered earth to you.
Love comes, and life is deified anew !
And hearts grow larger than their fortunes are.
The horizon lifts around, sublime and far,
With godlike breathing-space—an ample scope
For loftier life, and glorious ground for hope.

Turn, happy Lovers, turn on those below
A little of the light in which ye glow ;
A little of your sunshine round you shed,
And make our old world blossom where ye tread.
Bring back a little seed from Eden-bowers
To sow our fallows with immortal flowers.

Ah ! Nobles, what a chance is yours to be
The founders of a lordlier Chivalry !
And, with the proud old fire this people lead.
When they were weak, I threatened ; now I plead,
Give eyes to their blind strength, for great the
    need.

The *Word* of *Life* is well-nigh preached to
    death ;
The Flower of all Sweetness withereth
Crusht in the grip of many that handle it,
As though they thought Life would but yield its
    sweet
In giving up the breath.
               We want the Book
Translated into life, not the mere look
Of Life embalmed and shrouded in the Book.
We want the Word made Flesh to breathe once
    more
In likeness of the lineaments it wore
Living—the life indeed, quick in the lives
Of Fathers, Mothers, Children, Husbands, Wives.
We need that maiden life of Christ fulfilled
In Marriage—all its preciousness distilled.

We need the life itself—lived in the Home
On Week-days, ere the Sabbath-rest will come
To many a homeless hungerer for home.

We pray " *Thy Kingdom Come.*"   But not by prayer
Alone will it be built of breath in air.
In life thro' labour, must be brought to birth
The Kingdom ; as it is in heaven, on Earth.

The light that left Heaven centuries ago
Hath not yet reached dark myriads here below :
Your lives might be the lamp that bears this light,
Still burning, as the stars through all the night.
Because ye are lookt up to, they would mark
Your shining !
                    O, the spirits lying dark
To-day, as jewels waiting but the spark
Of splendour that to Love's dear smile is given,
To brighten with the best that brighten Heaven !
Look down, you Shining Ones, look kindly down,
And save them, set as jewels in your crown.

How beautiful upon the mountain height,
The feet of them that bring the Lowly light—

O'ershadowing, on wings of gentle Love,
The faults and failings that they soar above !
How beautiful the face of those whose smile
Doth make God's sunshine in the heart of Toil ;
In low, sick rooms a presence as of Health ;
The true Rich folk, in whom the Poor have wealth !
A beautiful life begets itself anew
In other lives, as perfume stealing through
The sense creates the flower to live again ;
Its spirit re-embodied in the brain.

Heartfull of shining love and singing hopes,
Come down where life, blind-folded, grovels and
    gropes.
We house the Poor to lie and die.   But give
Them room to stand in ; house the Poor to live ;
A little touch of clasping hands might prove
Mightiest of all the languages of Love.
Give them a glimpse of kindlier, sweeter grace,
And be the model of a nobler race—
The living Poem that we may not write ;
The picture that we cannot paint to sight ;
The music that we dream but do not get ;
The Statue marble never mirrored yet.

Come down, and meet them, fellow-man to man
So much we might do, as it seems, to span
The ancient gulf that severs Rich and Poor,
In which Christ threw Himself; for evermore
To show His sorrowing Poor that God hath not
Forgotten those He seemed to have forgot!

And the gulf closes not, and He doth reach
On either side a piteous hand to each:
One are they by the message that He gave;
One by the life He lived; one by His grave;
One by the tears He wept—the love—the pain;
And still they stand apart, and He is torn atwain.

Now while the Thrush upon the barest bough
Sits singing high in azure, telling how
The Spring-wind wanders where the Children go
A-violeting by the warm hedge-row;
Daily more rich the Sallow-palms unfold
And change their silver into sunny gold;
" *Good-bye, old Winter,*" the blue heavens laugh;
" *The flowers shall write you a kindly epitaph,*"
Far on a sea of Light the twinkling Lark
Is launched, and floating like a heaven-bound bark,

In which some happy spirit sails and sings,
And stirs us in a dream of waking wings,
With homeward yearnings, heavenward flutterings,
As all about the inner life there plays
A breath of bliss from out old innocent days,
Now, while the Spring mounts somewhere up the
    blue,
We bring our firstling flowers to offer you !
Violets, dim and tender ; glad Primroses,
That promise, ere the happy prospect closes,
Ye, hand in hand, through rosier days shall
    tread
Green earth, with richer glories garlanded ;
Where the wild Hyacinths, all a-dreaming, lean,
In peeps of deep sea-azure thro' the green ;
And Summer sets that Golden Age of hers
A-bloom, in mellow miles of yellow Furze ;
While, smiling down the distance, Autumn stands,
The ripened fruitage glowing in his hands.

And, if among the flowers some few appear
Sacred to woe, and leaning with the tear
Still in the eyes, I did but seek the leaf
Of Healing—gather Heartsease for your grief:

Nor are they tears, but rather drops of dew
From heaven, that hidden Love is looking through.

As, after death, our Lost Ones grow our Dearest,
So, after death, our Lost Ones come the nearest:
They are not lost in distant worlds above ;
They are our nearest link in God's own love—
The human hand-clasps of the Infinite,
That life to life, spirit to spirit knit !
They fill the rift they made, like veins of gold
In fire-rent fissures torture-torn of old !
With sweetness store the empty place they left,
As of wild honey in the rock's bare cleft.

In hidden ways they aid this life of ours,
As Sunshine lends a finger to the flowers,
Shadowed and shrouded in the Wood's dim heart,
To climb by while they push their grave apart.
They think of us at Sea, who are safe on Shore ;
Light up the cloudy coast we struggle for !
The ancient Terror of Eternity—
The dark destroyer, crouching in Life's sea
To wreck us—is thus Beaconed, and doth stand
As the Deliverer, with a lamp in hand.

We would not put them from us when we are sad ;
We will not shut them from us when we are glad ;
Nor thrust our Angel from the Marriage Feast,
Altho' he comes, not clothëd like the rest
In visible garment of a Wedding-Guest.

Now pray we.

　　　　　Lord of Life, look smiling down
Upon this Pair ; with choicest blessings crown
Their love ; the beauty of the Flower bring
Back to the bud again in some new spring !
Long may they walk the blessëd life together
With wedded hearts that still make golden weather,
And keep the chill of winter far aloof
With inward warmth when snow is on the roof ;
Wed in that sweet for ever of Love's kiss,
Like two rich notes made one in bridal bliss.

We would not pray that sorrow ne'er may shed
Her dews along the pathway they must tread :
The sweetest flowers would never bloom at all
If no least rain of tears did ever fall.
In joy the soul is bearing human fruit ;
In grief it may be taking divine root.

Come joy or grief, nestle them near to Thee
In happy love twin for eternity!
They take our Darling's place; long may they be
As glad and beautiful a hope as he
Hath left a bright and blessëd memory:
Their day fulfil the promise of his dawn—
That, as with Thee, he may with us live on.

AN ORPHAN FAMILY'S CHRISTMAS.

AN ORPHAN FAMILY'S CHRISTMAS.

I.

A BLITHE old Carle is Christmas;
   You cannot find his fellow;
Match me the hale red rose in his cheek,
   Or the heart so mild and mellow;
The glitter of glory in his eyes,
   While the Wassail-cup he quaffs,
Or the humour that twinkles about his wrinkles
   As helplessly he laughs.

Of all High-Tides 'tis Christmas
   Most richly crowns the year;
Right through the land there ripples and runs
   Its flood of merry good cheer.

Troops of friends come sailing down,
　　Making a pleasant din;
Fling open doors! set wide your hearts!
　　Christmas is coming in.

A happy time is Christmas,
　　We gather all at home,
And like the Christmas fairies,
　　With their pranks, our darlings come;
And gentle Sylvan Spirits hid
　　In holly-boughs they bring,
To grow into good Angels,
　　And bless our fairy-ring!

A jolly time is Christmas,
　　For Plenty's horn is poured;
Then flows the honey of the Sun,
　　Our fruits all summer hoard!
Merry men tall march up the hall:
　　They bear the meats and drinks;
And Wine, with all his hundred eyes,
　　Your hearty welcome winks.

A glorious time is Christmas;
　　Young hearts will slip the tether;

Lips moist and merry, all under the berry,
  Close thrillingly together.
A gracious time ! the poorest Poor
  Will make some little show,
As ailing infants, seeing the fun,
  Will do their best to crow !

And O the Fire of Christmas,
  That like some Norse God old,
Mounts his log up-chimney, and roars
  Defiance to the cold !
He challenges all out-of-doors :
  He wags his beard of flame ;
It warms your very heart to see
  Him glory in the game.

A hallowed time is Christmas,
  Of loftiest festival ;
For, eighteen hundred years ago,
  It opened Heaven to all.
'Twas then our Father, in his arms,
  The Blessèd Babe held forth
To win back wandering human love,
  And lure it up from Earth.

N

II.

But there are nooks in Poverty's dim world,
Where the high tide of richness never runs.
No drop of all its wealth for some who sit
And hear the river of bounty brimming by.
They see the Christmas shows of wealth and
    warmth,
At window, whilst at every door shut out!
The Plenty only flouts their poverty;
The music mocks them with its merriment;
They look into each passing face and find
No likeness of their own deep misery.

In one of these dark nooks, at Christmas time,
An Orphan family, with little fire,
And only light enough to see the gloom,
Together sat; two Sisters, and one Brother;
The youngest six years old; the eldest twelve;
An old Grandfather lying ill a-bed.
They knew that Christmas came, but not for them.
Thus had they often sat o' winter nights,
Shivering within, as the dark shuddered without,
And creeping close together for heart-warmth;

Poor unfledged nurslings with the Mother gone!
Knowing a Presence brooded over them,
In whose chill shadow they were pall'd and
    hooded;
So mournfully it kept the Mother's place!
Till flesh would creep as tho' about to leave
The spirit naked—bare to that cold breath
Which whispers of the grave—all lidless eye
To that appalling sight the helpless Dead
Lie looking on, in their amazement, dumb,
And petrified to marble! So they sat;
The Shadow in the house and on the heart;
The old Clock ticking thro' the lonely room,
With sounds that made the silence solemner,
And weird hands pointing to far other times;
Talking of merry Christmas coming in;
Of visionary futures, and old days,
With thoughts so far beyond their years! The life
In their young eyes gleamed supernaturally,
Betwixt the fire-shine, and the night-shadow,
As their old inmates of the heart stole forth
To walk and talk in the old ways once more.
And so, like those lorn pretty Babes i' the Wood,
That Robins buried when the talk was done,

They told each other stories ; sang their Hymns ;
By way of bribing the grim Solitude,
Not to look down upon them quite so dreadful !
Poor darlings, with no Father, and no Mother.

III.

Ay me, dear Sister, gentle Brother,
    How soft the thought of a Mother lies
    At heart ; how sweet in sound 'twill rise ;
And these poor Children had no Mother !

No Mother-arms, in secret nook
    To fold the sufferer to her breast,
    With love that never breaks its rest,
And Heartsease in her very look.

No Mother-wings to brood above
    The winter nest and keep them warm ;
    And shield them from the pitiless storm,
With the large shelter of her love.

No Mother's tender touch that brings
    A music from the harp of life,
    Like hovering heaven above the strife
And precious tremblings of the strings.

No Mother with her lap of love
    Each night for heads that bow in prayer;
    Dear hands that stroke the smiling hair,
And heart that pleads their cause above.

No Mother whose quick, wistful eye
    Will see the shadow of Danger near,
    And face, with love that casts out fear,
The blow that darkly hurtles by.

No Mother's smile ineffable,
    To stir the Angel in the bud,
    Till, into perfect womanhood,
The Flower blushes at the full.

No Mother! when the Darling One
    Bends with a grief that breaks the flower,
    To loose the sorrow in a shower,
And lift the sweet face to the sun.

No Mother's kiss of comfort near
  The River that Death overshades ;
  Or voice that, when the dim face fades,
Sounds on with solemn words of cheer.

Ay me, dear Sister, gentle Brother,
  How soft the thought of a Mother lies
  At heart ; how sweet in sound 'twill rise ;
And these poor Children had no Mother.

IV.

Yet, God is kind, and wondrous are His ways.
Affliction's hand, it seem'd, had, at a touch,
Awoke the Mother in the young Child-heart
Of little Martha, who had now become
A wee old woman at twelve years of age,
With many motherly ways.   Yea, God is kind.

The tiny Snowdrop braves the wintry blast ;
He tenderly protects its confidence
That lifts the venturous head, safe in His hand :
And Martha, in her loneliness of earth,
And such a dearth of human fellowship,
And such companionship with solitude,

Had found a way of looking up to Heaven :
And oft I think that God in heaven smiled :
Holding his hand about her little life,
As one that shields a candle from the wind.
She had the faith to feel him nearest, when
The world is farthest off; and, in this faith,
Her spirit went on wings, or, hand-in-hand
With Love that digs below the deepest grave,
And Hope that builds above the highest stars.

In the old days before their sorrow came,
And vast Eternity oped twice to them,
And each time, following the lightning-flash,
They groped in darkness for a Parent gone,
She was the merriest of merry souls ;
The gay heart laughing in her loving eyes ;
The peeping rose-bud crimsoning her cheek ;
There was as quick a spirit in her feet,
As now had pass'd into her toiling fingers,
That match the Mother's heart with Father's
    hands
In their unwearied working for the rest.
In those old days the Father made a song
About his little maid, and sang it to her.

V.

"*It is a merry Maiden,*
  With spirits light as air ;
While others go heart-laden,
  And make the most of care,
She trips along with laughter :
Old Care may hobble after.

"*A sunbeam straight from heaven,*
  She dances in my room ;
The gladdest thing e'er given
  To cheer a heart or home,
My stream of life may darkle ;
She makes the brighter sparkle.

"*Her smile is like the Morning*
  That turns the mist to pearls ;
All thought of sadness scorning,
  She shakes her sunny curls ;
And, with her merry glancing,
Sets every heart a-dancing."

VI.

BUT now the Maid was changed; for she had
    been
With Sorrow in its chilly sanctuary;
Her look was paler, for it had been toucht
With that white stillness of the winding-sheet,
That smile forlornly sweet upon the face
When left for ever widowed of the soul.
Henceforth her life went softly all its days
As if she felt the Grave-turf underfoot.
Her beauty was more spiritual; not aged
Or worn; less colour, but more light.
It was a brier-rose beauty, tremulous
With tenderest dew-drop purity of soul.

I've often seen how well their beauty wears
Whose sufferings are for others, not for Self;
How long they keep a fair unfurrow'd face,
Whose tears are luminous with healing love,—
The pearly cars that bring good spirits down
To water and enrich their special flowers,—
And do not come from cares that kill the heart;

These sere no bloom ; they leave no snaky trail.
So Martha kept her face, and might have been
The younger sister of that lily Maid,
The loveable Elaine of Astolat.

VII.

WE write the tale of Heroes in the blood
They shed when dying where they nobly stood ;
And the red letters gloriously bloom
To light the warrior to a loftier doom.
But there are battles where no cheers arise,
And no flags wave before the fading eyes ;
Heroes of whom the wide world never hears ;
Their story only writ in Woman's tears.
Yet that invisible ink shall surely shine
Brightest in Heaven, and verily divine.
And when God closes our world's blotted book,
To cast it in the fire with awful look,
It was so badly written, leaf on leaf
Thus lived might touch the Father's heart with
    grief.

And this Child-Mother's life may yield one story
That shall be told among the first in glory.

Her busy love and thoughtful care are such,
The others do not miss the Mother much.
From dawn to dark her presence lights the place
With many a gleam of reliquary grace.
Their few poor things in seemly order stand,
Bright as with last touch of the Parent's hand.
The clothes are mended, and the house is kept
Clean as of old; bravely hath Martha stepped
In Mother's footprints; her wee feet have tried
Their best to track the Parent's larger stride.
With household work her little hands are hard,
Her arms are chill'd, her knees with kneeling
        scarred :
Dusty her hair that might have richly roll'd
With warm Venetian glow of Titian's gold.
Great-hearted little woman ! she toils still,
Tho' the Grandfather, lying old and ill,
To her twin troubles adds a heavier third,
She works on without one complaining word.

VIII.

AND once a year she has her holiday;
One day of airy life in fairyland.
When young leaves open large their palms to catch
The gold and silver of the sun and shower;
Shy Beauty pusheth back her glittering hood,
To peep with her flower face; the Silver Birk
Shakes out her hair full-length against the blue;
The Fir puts forth her timid finger-tips,
Like shrinking damsel trying a cold stream
In which she comes to bathe.

　　　　　　　　　In merry green woods
She rambles where the blue wild hyacinths
Smile with their soft dream-haze in tender shade:
Above, the lightsome dance of gladsome green;
Below, the whispering sweetness of the wood;
Birds singing, as for love of her, all round:
Or, by the Brook that turns some stray sunbeam
To a crooked scimitar of wavy gold,
Then to itself laughs at the elfish work!
With her large eyes, and eager leaping looks,
At Nature's living picture-page she glowers,

And gets some colour in her own pale life.
Then home, with kindled cheek, when Eve's one
    Star
Stands, waiting on the threshold of the night,
In lively expectation of all heaven.

IX.

HOME when the happy day is done,
    Home comes my little Maid;
Her pleasure—golden in the sun—
    Now dewy in the shade.
Thoughts of the day will hover and bless
Her sleep with sacred balminess.

Thro' shutting eve the stars all peep,
    But still there comes no night;
'Tis but the Day hath fall'n asleep
    And smiles in dreams of light.
And Martha feels the heart of Love
Beat on in silent stars above.

X.

TO-NIGHT they sit with sadder, lonelier thoughts
Than ever ; closer comes the Wolf of Want,
And darklier falls their shadow of Orphanhood.
For now the old man keeps his bed, and seems
Death-stricken, with his face of ghastly grey ;
His life all crowded in cold glittering eyes
Watching the least light movement that is made.
The Boy, a blithe and sunny godsend, gay
As singing fountain springing in their midst,
With loving spirit leaping to the light,
Is down at heart to-night, and sad and still.
While Dora, in whose purple-lighted eyes
There seems the shadow of a rain-cloud near,
With but a faint shine of the cheery heart ;
She longs to fly away and be at rest,
And gives her wishes wings in measured words
That win strange pathos from her sweet young
     voice.

" *Come to the Better Land, that Angels know ;*
They walk in glory, shining as they go !

The King in all His beauty takes the least
To sit beside Him at the eternal feast."
Thus sings the voice that calls me night and day.
  " This is a weary world,
   Come, come, come away !
  Ah, 'tis a dreary world,
   Come, come away."

"From old heart-ache, and weariness, and pain—
Sorrows that sigh, and hopes that soar in vain—
Come to the Loved and Lost who are now the Blest;
They dwell in regions of Eternal rest."
Thus sings the voice that calls me night and day.
  " This is a weary world,
   Come, come, come away!
  Ah, 'tis a dreary world,
   Come, come away."

" Here all things change; the warmest hearts grow
 cold;
The young head droops and dims its glorious gold;
Where Love his pillow hath made on Beauty's breast,
The creatures of the Grave will make their nest."

Thus sings the voice that calls me night and day.

> *" This is a weary world,*
> *Come, come, come away !*
> *Ah, 'tis a dreary world,*
> *Come, come away."*

" The dear eyes where each morning rose our light,
Soon darken with their last eternal night;
The heart that beat for us, the hallowed brow
That bowed to bless, are cold and silent now."
Thus sings the voice that calls me night and day.

> *" This is a weary world,*
> *Come, come, come away !*
> *Ah, 'tis a dreary world,*
> *Come, come away."*

" Nor fear the Grave, that door of Heaven on Earth;
All changed and beautiful ye shall come forth,
As from the cold dark cloud the winter showers
Go underground to dress, and come forth Flowers."
Thus sings the voice that calls me night and day.

> *" This is a weary world,*
> *Come, come, come away !*
> *Ah, 'tis a dreary world,*
> *Come, come away."*

" *Come to the Better Land, that Angels know ;*
They walk in glory, shining as they go !
The King in all His beauty takes the least
To sit beside Him at the eternal feast."
Thus sings the voice that calls me night and day.
    " *This is a weary world,*
      Come, come, come away !
    Ah, 'tis a dreary world,
      Come, come away."

XI.

"NAY, Sister," says the cheery Martha, "though
Our lot be sad, your strain's too sorrowful !
We cannot spare you yet.   Nor must we stoop
To make our Burthen heavier ; hear me, love.

   " *A little flower so lowly grew,*
     So lonely was it left,
  That Heaven lookt like an eye of blue
     Down in its rocky cleft.

" *What could the little Flower do*
    In such a darksome place,
But try to reach that eye of blue,
    And climb to kiss Heaven's face?

" *And there's no life so lone and low*
    But strength may still be given
From narrowest lot on earth to grow
    The straighter up to Heaven."

Again she sang, and set them singing too.

" *When He was with us, our Saviour said,*
    Suffer the Children to come unto me:
Still I see Him, with arms outspread,
    Waiting to gather us round his knee.
And tho' there's room for all the rest,
I think He loves the Little Ones best.

" *Here we are poorest of God's Poor,*
    Toiling for bread from day to day,
But laid up in Heaven a treasure is sure,
    While Money is round and rolls away.
And tho' there's room for all the rest,
I think He loves the Little Ones best.

" *Little hearts make merry, and sing*
How his love to Children warms !
Little voices ripple and ring—
How he takes them in his arms !
And tho' there's room for all the rest,
I think He loves the Little Ones best."

XII.

THEN, silent Leonard lifted up his look,
Bright as a Daisy when the dews have dried ;
A sudden thought struck all the sun in his face.
" *Martha and Dora, I know what I'll do !*
I'll write a Letter to our Saviour ; He
Will help us if we put our trust in Him."
The sisters smiled upon him thro' their tears.

This was the Letter little Leonard wrote.

" *Dear, beautiful Lord Jesus,*
Christmas is drawing near ;
Its many shining sights we see,
Its merry sounds we hear,

With presents for good Children,
  I know Thou art going now,
From house to house with Christmas trees,
  And lights on every bough.

" I pray thee, holy Jesus,
  To bring one tree to us,
All aglow with fruits of gold,
  And leaves all luminous.
We have no Mother, and, where we live,
  No Christmas gifts are given;
We have no Friends on earth, but thou
  Art our good friend in Heaven.

" My Sisters, gentle Jesus,
  They hide the worst from me;
But I have ears that sometimes hear,
  And eyes that often see.
Poor Martha's cloak is worn threadbare,
  Poor Dora's boots are old;
And neither of them strong like me,
  To stand the wintry cold.

" But most of all, Lord Jesus,
  Grandfather is so ill;

'Tis very sad to hear him moan,
And startling when he's still.
Ah ! well I know, Lord Jesus,
If thou would'st only come,
He'd look, and rise, and leave his bed,
As Lazarus left his tomb.

" Forget us, not, Lord Jesus,
I and my sisters dear ;
We love thee ! when thou wert a Child,
Had we been only near,
And seen thee lying, bonny babe,
In manger or in stall,
Thou should'st have had a home with us ;
We would have given thee all."

· XIII.

THE Letter sign'd and seal'd, their prayers are said,
And Martha lights the younger Bairns to bed.
With all a Mother's heart she bends above
Their rest, her eyes filled with a Mother's love.

For soon their voices cease; life fades away
Into its quiet nest, till morrow-day:
As the lake-lilies shut their leaves of light
When down the gloom descends the hush of night,
In fear of what is passing, bow the head
Beneath the water, they shrink down in bed!
But soon the Angel Sleep doth smile all fear
Away with wooing whispers at the ear;
And they will ope at morn eyes bathed in bliss;
Their faces fresh from the good Angel's kiss.
But Martha sleeps not yet; now they are gone,
Brave little woman, she must still work on,
And watch, to-night, for Grandfather is worse,
She thinks, with no one near, save her for nurse.

XIV.

'TIS very sad to hear a man so old,
Talk of *his* mother who, beneath the mould,
Has lain an age, and see him weep young tears,
That have to pierce the crust of seventy years.
He turns and turns, incapable of rest,
Toss'd on the billow that heaves in brain and
    breast;

A life that beats with all too weak a wave
To land him on the other side the Grave!
The old man mutters in his broken dream.

" *Last night I wander'd in a world of moan;*
I saw a white Soul going all alone,
   Over the white snows of eternity;
   I follow'd far, and follow'd fast to see
The face, and lo, it was my own."

And now he muses by some weird sea-side.

" *The tide is a-making its bonny Death-bed;*
The white sea-maidens rise ready to wed;
Nearer and nearer, unveiling their charms,
They toss for their lovers, long, shadowy arms!
Dancing with other-world music and motion,
Brides of dead Sailors; the Beauties of Ocean.

" *Wave after wave my worn, old Bark has toss'd;*
One moment saved, another it seem'd lost
For ever, still it righted from each blow;
But the great wave is coming on me now!
I see it towering high above the rest;
A world of eyes in its white glittering crest;

See how it climbs, calm in its might, and curls
Ready to clasp me in the wildering whirls.
And when it bursts, in darkness, for last breath,
I shall be fighting, grappled fast with Death."

He sees an Image of Martha now, with dim
Wet eyes ; it moves in brightness far from him.

> " *I am like the hoary Mountain,*
> *Grey with years, and very old ;*
> *And your life, a sprightly fountain,*
> *Springs, and leaves me lone and cold ;*
> *Dancing, glancing on its way,*
> *Down the valleys warm and gay.*

> " *There you go, Dear, singing, sparkling,*
> *I can see your dawn begin ;*
> *While the night, around me darkling,*
> *With its death-dews, shuts me in—*
> *Hear you singing on your way*
> *To the full and perfect day."*

The suffering passes into weariness ;
The weariness fades into kind content ;

Faintly the tired heart flutters into stillness,
And he has done with Age, and Want, and Illness.

Gently he passed ; the little Maiden wept ;
Sank down o'erwearied by the dead, and slept,
With such a heavenly lustre in her face,
You might have fancied Angels in the place :
Companions thro' the day of our delight,
That watch as wingëd Sentries all the night.

XV.

NEXT day a group of serious silent men
Found a *Dead Letter* with strange life in it ;
It was addressed to *Jesus Christ in Heaven.*
It call'd up their old hearts into their eyes,
For lofty meeting in a touch of tears.
At length it reached the Lady Marian.
And the Boy's letter had not missed its mark.

The child had call'd on Christ, and lo, He came :
In spirit loving, helpful, as of old !
In person of the Lady Marian ;

One of those representatives of His
Who help to make the Poor believe in Him :
Believe Him once a dweller on our earth
Because He hath some living likeness yet.

XVI.

THIS is my Lady Marian:
She walks our world, a Shining one !
A Woman with an Angel-face,
Sweet gravity, and tender grace ;
And where she treads this earth of ours,
Heaven blossoms into smiling flowers.
  This is the Lady Marian.

One of the spirits that walk in white !
Many dumb hearts that sit in night,
Her presence know, just as the Birds
Know Morning, murmuring cheerful words.
Where Life is darkest, she doth move
With influence as of visible Love.
  This is the Lady Marian.

Her coming all your being fills
With a balm-breath from heaven's hills :
And in her face the light is mild
As tho' the heart within her smiled,
And in her bosom sat to sing
The spirit of immortal Spring.
　　　　This is the Lady Marian.

One of God's treasurers for the Poor !
She keepeth open heart and door.
That heart a holy well of wealth,
Brimming life-waters, quick with health ;
That door an opening you look through,
To find God our side of Heaven's blue.
　　　　This is the Lady Marian.

" *We shall not mend the world; we try,*
And lo, our work is vain ! " they cry.
With her pathetic look, she hears ;
You see the wounded soul bleed tears ;
But toward the dark she sets her face,
And calmly keeps her onward pace.
　　　　This is the Lady Marian.

True picture of the Master of old !
Touches of likeness manifold !
The human sweetness in His face ;
Large love that would a world embrace ;
His heavenly pity in her eyes,
And all the soul of sacrifice.
   This is the Lady Marian.

XVII.

FROM out the blackness that took shape in Her,
Came Lady Marian on Christmas Eve,
Quick with maternal tenderness of soul,
Her starry smile so radiant through their night,
Her hands brimful of help, as was her heart
With yearnings to arise and go when first
She read the letter little Leonard sent
In his confiding simpleness of faith.
And Martha knows that their worst days are done ;
In Dora's rich sad eyes a merry light
Soon dances ! Lady Marian will be
A Mother, sent of God, to all the three.

A trembling prayer had shook the Tree of Life,
And, golden, out of heaven the fruitage falls
Into the children's lap direct from God.

XVIII.

THE Master call'd a little Child,
    And placed it in their midst, to show
    The clearest mirror men could know,
In which the face of Faith e'er smiled:

A little Child, with eye unworn,
    Whose heart goes straightway for the light,
    Like buds that put forth all their might
To start up heavenward soon as born:

A little Child, that even in play
    The nearest path to heaven walks;
    And in its innocent brightness talks
With God in the old wondrous way:

Friends of a failing faith, when your
   Lighthouses of eternal life
   Hold trembling lamps across the strife,
And darken, darken hour by hour:

While higher climb the waves that drench:
   And on the rocks the breakers roar:
   And Light in Heaven opes no new door,
 And higher climb the waves that quench:

When timid souls that sail the sea
   Of Time are fearful lest yon band
   Of Cloud should not be solid Land,
When they step in Eternity,—

And faint hearts flutter 'twixt a nest
   That is not sealed to wind and wet,
   And one that is not ready yet,
With wandering wings, and find no rest:

Our Heaven-scalers in the dust
   Sit, with their hopes dead or discrown'd;
   Their splendid dreams all shiver'd round
And broken every reed of trust:

The Sheep are scatter'd, sore distress'd;
   Their Shepherd miss with many alarms;
   While the young Lambs can feel His arms
Enfold them safely to His breast:

I'll sit me down, no more beguiled
   By those who are too serpent-wise;
   And seek my Saviour through the eyes
And pure heart of a little Child.

Christ, give me but this little one's grace,
   With faith to feel in darkest night,
   How the good Father's heart of light
With that mild radiance fills Thy face.

A POET'S LOVE-LETTER.

P

A POET'S LOVE-LETTER.

YOU ask me, Friend, to tell you of my Wife !
    And on what stair or landing-place of life
I met, as 'twere, God's Angel coming down,
Or mine ascending, for her marriage crown ?

I say you sooth, however strange it seem,
The first time that I saw her was in dream :
A vision of the night did clearly glass
Her living lineaments. I saw her pass
Smiling, as those may smile who feel they hold
At heart safe-hidden, secret fold on fold,
The sweetest love that ever was untold.
And as it went the Vision flasht on me
A moment's look ; a lifetime's memory.
But little could I dream that this should prove
The whole wide world's one lady of my love.

I had never seen that face or form, and yet
I knew them both by daylight when we met.

Blind World! to pass, and pass my darling by,
My lily of the vale, where she did lie
Snug in her own green leaves, and never see
The flower veiled and waiting there for me,
With cloudy fragrance all about her curled ;
And yet my blessings on thee, O blind World !
It is so sweet to find with one's own eyes,
Led by divine good-hap, to her surprise,
Our Perdita, our Princess in disguise !
The eye that finds must bring the power to see ;
(Says Goethe's doctrine, comforting to me !)
And now she's found, the world would give me much
Could I but tell it of another such.

Is she an Angel ?
                Let us not forget,
My Friend, that WE are scarcely Angels yet.
At least my modest soul would not be pledged
To call itself an Angel fully fledged :
Flesh is so frail ! nor am I very sure
Of being, in spirit, altogether pure !

Snags of old broken sins torment me still
With pains that Death itself will hardly kill.
If not an Angel, let the truth be told,
I have not grasped the glitter—missed the
    Gold.
And lucky is the man who gets the gold,
Refined and fitted for the marriage mould !
Still happier who can keep it pure to bear
The finer features of immortal wear.
She is of Angel-stuff; but I'm afraid
The Angels are not given us ready-made :
In other worlds, this wife of mine may be
The perfect public Angel all may see ;
At present she's a private one for me—
My household deity of Common Things,
That into lowly ways a beauty brings,
Just as the grass comes creeping, making bright
And blessëd, with its ripples of delight
And quiet smiles, all pathways dim and bare.

Is she a Beauty ?
          Well, I will not swear
A thousand beauties with her beauty blend ;
A thousand graces on her Grace attend ;

Or that she is so pitilessly fair
Each passer-by must turn, or stop, or stare,
And he on whom she looks feels instantly
As one that springs from dust to deity.
Nor can I sing of outer symbols now—
The swan-white stately neck ; the snow-white brow ;
The lip's live rose ; the head superbly crowned ;
Eyes, that when fathomed, farthest heaven is
    found !
I chose for worth, not show, nor chose for them
Who want the casket richer than the gem.

That Wife is poor, whate'er her dower may be,
Who hath no beauty save what all may see :
No mystery of the human and divine;
No other face to unveil within the shrine,
Up-lighted only for one worshipper,
And to one love alone familiar :
No veil to lift from the familiar face
Daily, and show the unfamiliar grace.
Eyes shine for others, but divinely dim
And dewy do they grow only for him !
And her dear face transfigured he doth find
All mirror to the marvel in his mind !

The beauty worn by Bird and Butterfly
Lives on the outside, lustrous to the eye :
But still as nobler grow hue, form, and face.
More inward is shy Beauty's dwelling-place.
And there's a beauty fashioned in the mould
Transmitted from the Beautiful of old,
That from some family-face its best doth win :
But my love's beauty cometh from within ;
The loveliness of love made visible,
To feature which the sculptor Form is dull :
Not the mere charms of cheek, or chin, or lip,
That vanish on a week's acquaintanceship ;
But that crown-beauty which we cannot clasp,
The beauty that eludes Death's own grave-grasp.

At forty, what we seek for in a Wife
Is a calm haven amid seas of strife :
One fresh green summit in the waste of life,
That gathers dew of heaven and tenderly
Turns it to healing drops for you or me ;
A spring of freshness in the desert sand ;
A palm for shadow in a weary land ;
A being that doth not dwell so far apart
That we can find no entrance save at heart ;

One that at equal step with us may walk,
And kiss at equal stature in our talk;
And scale the loftiest life, still arm-in-arm,
As well as nestle in the valleys warm.

And here's my Rest, where sun and shadow meet
O'erhead, the small flowers budding at my feet;
Green picnic places peeping from the wood,
Where you may meet the spirit of Robin Hood
Crossing the moonlight at the old deer-chase;
A brooding Dove the Spirit of the place;
Gleams of the Graces at their bath of dew;
An earthly pleasaunce; heaven trembling thro';
My Darling sitting with her hand in mine,
Here, where mid the lush grass the large-eyed
    kine
Ruminant, stolid, statelily behold
The milky plenty and the blossoming gold:
And with glad laugh the tiny buttercup
Its beaker of delight brimful holds up;
And prodigally glorified, the mead
Is all aglow with red-ripe sorrel-seed,
And quick with smells that make one long to be
A-gathering sweets, bloom-buried utterly.

The sylvan world's old royalties around
With all their summer beauty newly crown'd :
Broad beeches, that have caught alive the swirl
O' the wind-wave—shaped it in their branches' curl ;
Proud oaks, from head to foot all feudal yet ;
And whispering pines, that have in worship met,—
Their delicate Gothic sharp against the shine
Of sunset heaven's honeyed hyaline—
As dark and still and plumëd, as the Hearse
Of day's departed glory, are those Firs
When Venus, glowing in the Lift above,
Laughs down on lovers with the eye of Love,
Luminous in her loveliness, as though
The Goddess' self were coming from the glow.

I brought my Love here happy months ago,
Her winter prison, amid miles of snow.
Poor bird ! she felt that she was caged at last,
Her forest far away, its freedom past :
Her eyes made mournful search, mine laughed to
    see,
She would have flown, and knew not where to flee.
The little wedding ring had grown, a round
Large hoop about our lives, and we were bound !

Useless was all petitionary quest,
No outlet !—so she nestled in my breast ;
And may we always be as wise, my dear,
When things look dark around, or foes are near.

And now the fragrant summer-tide hath come
And isled us in a sea of leaf and bloom.
And now the tremulous sweetness, restless grace,
Have settled down to brood in the dear face
That lightens by me, fair and privet-pale,
Soft in the shadow of the bridal veil :
The sunny sparkle of Southern radiance
That in her English blood doth bicker and dance,
Hath steadied to the still and sacred glow
Which hath more inner life than outer show.

So many are the mishaps and the griefs
In marriage, like Beau Brummel's Neckerchiefs ;
Armfuls of failure for one perfect tie !
And *have we hit it ?* do you say or sigh.

Time was when life in triumph would have run,
And faster than the fields catch fire o' the sun,

Or light takes shape and feature in the flowers,
My answer would have blossomed with the hours.
I should have felt the buds begin to blow
With my love-warmth, another dawn to glow;
Heard all the bells in heaven ring quite plain
Because young blood went singing through my
    brain :
Like vernal impulses the verses came ;
My soul on tiptoe and my words a-flame.
I should have sung that we had reached the land
Where milk and honey flow o'er golden sand,
And that far *El Dorado* we had found
Where nothing less than nuggets glad the ground.
But 'tis no more the lyric life of youth,
When fancy seemëd truer than all truth,
And standing in that dawn, the sun of love
Hung dewy rainbows on each web we wove,
And to the leap o' the blood we felt it given
To scale the tallest battlements of heaven ;
Poor was the prize of wisdom's proudest dower
Beside that glory of the flesh in flower !

And now I cannot sing my ladye's praise,
Lark-like, as in the morning of those days

When at a touch the song would upward start,
And, half in heaven, empty all the heart.
'Tis August with me now and harvest-heat,
And in the nest the silence is so sweet ;
Moreover, love is such a bosom thing,
In words its nestling nearnesses take wing ;
Nor flower of speech could ever yet express
The married sweetness or the homeliness ;
We cannot fable the ineffable ;
The tongue is tied too, with the heart at full :
Music may hint it with her latest breath,
But fails ;—her heaven is only reached through
    Death.

The stirring of the sap in bole and bough—
Mere feeling—will not set me singing now !
I thank my God for all that he hath given
And ope the windows of my soul to heaven ;
I think, in bowed and very humble mood,
I must be better, He hath been so good.
So would I journey to the land above,
Clothed with humility and crowned with love.

I look no more Without, and think to win
The treasures that are only found Within ;

And, after many years, have grown too wise
To search our world for some lost paradise;
Or feel unhappy should we chance to miss
The next life's possibilities in this.
'Tis here we follow—but hereafter find
The goal all-golden miraged in the mind.
That Age of Gold behind us, and the Isles
Where dwelt the Blessëd are but as the smiles
Reflected from a heaven that onward lies,
The Gold of sundown caught in orient skies.

And yet, if any bit of Eden bloom
In this old world, 'tis in the WEDDED HOME.
And, what a wonder-world of novel life
Do these two range thro', hand-in-hand, as Wife
And Husband; in one flesh two spirits paired;
Their joys all doubled, all their sorrows shared:
Two spirits blending in one heavenward spire,
That soars up fragrant from an altar fire;
Two halves in one perfection wed to prove
The shaped Idea of immortal love!

We cannot see Love with our mortal sight,
But lo! the singing Angels come some night

To bring His tiny image in the Child
Wherewith from out the darkness He hath smiled;
The tender voice whereby the All-loving breaks
His silence, and in human fashion speaks;
The gentle hand put forth to draw us near
The heart of life whose pulse is beating here.
Tho' seldom do we guess, so dim our eyes,
That God comes down in such a simple guise,
And yet of such the kingdom of Heaven is;
Thro' them the next world is revealed in this!

And how they come to us to bring us back
What we have lost along the dusty track:
The sweetness of the dawn, the early dew,
And tender green, and heaven's unclouded blue;
The treasures that we dropped upon the ground,
And they, in following after us, have found!

Ah, Love, my life is not so bare of leaf
But we can find a nest for shelter if
The bounteous heavens should bless us from above
And in our branches cradle some wee dove.
Nor will my darling lack a touch still warm
To finish that fine sculpture of her form;

For if Love dwell in me, the Angel-Elf
Shall kiss her to some likeness of himself.

At the hill-top I reach my resting place,
To find clear heaven—feel it face to face;
Firm footing after all the weary slips,
To hold the cup unshaken at the lips.
The meaning of my life grows clear at last,
And all my troubles smile back now they're past :
The clouds put on a glory to mine eyes,
My sorrows were my Saviour in disguise :
And I have walked with angels unawares,
And upward mounted, climbing over cares,
A little nearer to the home above.
Here let me rest in the good Father's love
Embodied in these arms embracing me,
Serenely as the sea-flowers in deep sea.

'Tis true, just as we feel our foreheads crowned,
And all so glorious grows the prospect round,
It seems one stride might launch us on heaven's
        wave,
Thenceforth our steps go downward to the grave.

What then? I would not rest till spirit rust,
And I am undistinguishable dust :
And if Love bring no second spring to me,
This is the fore-feel of a spring to be ;
If no new Dawn, yet in the evening hours,
Freshly bedewed, more sweetly smell the flowers ;
And round my path the glow of love hath made
Gentle illumination for the shade.

Something, dear Lord, thou hast for me to say,
Or wherefore draw me toward the springs of
        day,
And make my face with happiness to shine
By softly placing this dear hand in mine
Even while I stretch it to Thee thro' the dark :
A something that shall shine aloft and mark
Thy goodness and my gratitude upon
This Mount Transfiguration when I'm gone ?
If thou hast set my foot on firmer ground,
Lord, let me show what helper I have found ;
If Thou hast touched me with thy loftier light,
Lord, let me turn to those that walk in night
And climb with more at heart than they can bear,
Tho' but a twinkle through their cloud of care.

Only a grain of sand my life may be,
But let it sparkle, Lord, with light of Thee!

I ask not that my verse should break in bloom
With flowers, to crown my love or wreathe my
    tomb;
Nor do I seek the laurel for my brow,
But only that above my grave may grow
Some sunny grains of thine immortal seed
That may be garnered up for human need—
In Bread of Life on which poor souls may feed!

Of late my life hath nestled more at root,
Making new sap, I trust, for future fruit:
Lord, sun my harvest, set it ripening
With sheaves in autumn thick as leaves in spring!
It is my prayer at night, my dream by day,
To write the poem of the Poor.   I pray
Thee let me have my one supreme desire,
To fill some earthly facts with heavenly fire;
Give voice to their dumb world before I die;
Their patient pain more piteous than a cry!
Let me work now, while all eternity
With its large-seeming leisure waits for me.

Q

HYMNS, AND OTHER LYRICS.

(SOME OF WHICH WERE WRITTEN TO BE SUNG BY CHILDREN.)

AT EVENTIDE.

THOU infinitely merciful !
    Thy garment's hem in prayer we pull ;
Bringing our burdens on our knees,
We take the hand that lends release :
Turn on us one forgiving look,
Before this day shall close its book.

So yearningly we seek thy face
When darkness is our dwelling-place.
Our foolish hearts, that daily roam,
Would nightly nestle with Thee at Home.
Be with us Here, and grant that we
Hereafter, Lord, may be with Thee !

Father! our inmost parts lie bare
To Thine own purifying air;
We spread our stains out in Thy sight;
O, Sun of Pureness, turn them white:
And make our spirits clear as dew
For thine own Self to lighten through.

Send down the Comforter, we plead, ·
For all who are in bitter need;
Let homeless Hagars find, we pray,
Some well of succour by the way:
With the Angel of Thy Presence bless
Poor wanderers in the wilderness.

God keep our darlings safe this night,
Tho' scattered, *one* still in Thy sight!
Lead on, by many ways, and past
All perils, till we join at last:
With us the broken links! with Thee
The circle perfect endlessly.

Now take us, Father, to Thy breast,
And still all troubled thoughts to rest;

Thy watch and ward about us keep,
That tired souls may smile asleep,
And, having been in heaven awhile,
May wake to-morrow with Thy smile!

OUT OF THE DEPTHS.

S O dark the way, I cannot see :
    O, somewhere-smiling face Divine,
Look down and make my night to shine !
So dark the way, I cannot see.
Dear Jesus, let me lean on Thee !

All night I stumble gropingly,
   Seeking the door in some blank wall,
   That shuts me from the light, and call
And listen, listen hopingly.
Dear Jesus, let me lean on Thee !

My burden bows me to the knee;
  O Lord, 'tis more than I can bear.
  Didst Thou not come our load to share?
My burden bows me to the knee.
Dear Jesus, let me lean on Thee !

The Deeps will surely swallow me ;
  I cry with fainting strength: the waves
  Are gaping round in open graves:
The Deeps will surely swallow me.
Dear Jesus, let me lean on Thee !

Far off, so far, the Heavens be,
  With their wide arms ! and I would prove
  The close warm-beating heart of Love.
But so far off the Heavens be :
Dear Jesus, let me lean on Thee !

Father in Heaven, we cannot see
  Thy face, nor grasp the spirit-hand
  That leads us to the Unseen Land ;
But trustingly, tho' tremblingly,
Dear Jesus, let me lean on Thee !

One smile, and all my fears would flee :
   One whisper, and the storm would cease ;
   And I should know Thee in the peace ;
The door would ope; no dark could be.
Dear Jesus, let me lean on Thee !

JERUSALEM THE GOLDEN.

JERUSALEM the Golden !
   I weary for one Gleam
Of all thy glory folden
   In distance and in dream !
My thoughts, like Palms in Exile,
   Climb up to look and pray
For a glimpse of thy dear Country
   That lies so far away !

Jerusalem the Golden !
   Methinks each flower that blows,
And every bird a-singing
   Of thee some secret knows ;

I know not what the Flowers
 Can feel, or Singers see,
But all these summer raptures
 Seem prophecies of thee.

Jerusalem the Golden !
 When Sunset's in the West,
It seems thy gate of glory,
 Thou City of the Blest !
And Midnight's starry torches
 Thro' intermediate gloom,
Are waving with our welcome
 To thy Eternal Home !

Jerusalem the Golden !
 Where loftily they sing,
O'er pain and sorrows olden
 For ever triumphing ;
Lowly may be the portal
 And dark may be the door,
The Mansion is Immortal—
 God's palace for His Poor !

Jerusalem the Golden !
 There all our Birds that flew,—

Our Flowers but half unfolden,
　　Our Pearls that turned to dew,—
And all the glad life-music,
　　Now heard no longer here,
Shall come again to greet us
　　As we are drawing near.

Jerusalem the Golden !
　　I toil on, day by day ;
Heart-sore each night with longing,
　　I stretch my hands and pray,
That mid thy leaves of Healing,
　　My soul may find her nest ;
Where the Wicked cease from troubling—
　　The Weary are at rest !

THE ONLY ONE.

WITH tired feet, o'er thorny ground,
My spirit made its quest;
On wearied wing it wandered round,
But could not find its nest;
Till at my Saviour's feet I found
At last my Only Rest!

I went the downward way of Doom,
With those that walk in night;
I stumbled on from tomb to tomb
Of Joys that lured my sight;
Until He touched me thro' the gloom
And smiled—my Only Light!

All gleams of glory, shapes of grace,
   My Saviour shines above :
He sits in Heaven for brooding-place :
   He comes down like a Dove !
I look up in His pitying face
   And know my Only Love !

O sweet the touch of hearts, and sweet
   The tie of Child and Wife !
And blessëd is the home where meet
   True souls that shut out strife ;
But nestling at my Saviour's feet,
   I know the Only Life.

POOR MAN'S SUNDAY.

THE merry Birds are singing,
   And from the fragrant sod
The Spirits of a thousand flowers
   Go sweetly up to God:
While in His holy temple
   We meet to praise and pray
With cheerful voice, and grateful heart,
   This Summer Sabbath Day!

We thank thee, Lord, for one day
   To look Heaven in the face!
The Poor have only Sunday;
   The sweeter is the grace,

'Tis then they make the music
 That sings their week away.
O, there's a sweetness infinite
 In the Poor Man's Sabbath Day !

'Tis as a burst of sunshine,
 A tender fall of rain,
That set the barest life a-bloom ;
 Make old hearts young again.
The dry and dusty roadside
 With smiling flowers is gay ;
'Tis open Heaven one day in seven,
 The Poor Man's Sabbath Day !

'Tis here the weary Pilgrim
 Doth reach his House of Ease !
That blessèd House, called " Beautiful,"
 And that soft Chamber, " Peace."
The River of Life runs through his dream
 And the leaves of Heaven are at play ;
He sees the Golden City gleam,
 This shining Sabbath Day !

Take heart, ye faint and fearful,
 Your cross with courage bear ;

R

So many a face now tearful
  Shall shine in glory there;
Where all the sorrow is banisht,
  The tears are wiped away;
And all eternity shall be
  An endless Sabbath Day!

Ah! there are empty places,
  Since last we mingled here!
There will be missing faces
  When we meet another year!
But, heart to heart, before we part,
  Now altogether pray
That we may meet in Heaven, to spend
  The Eternal Sabbath Day!

THE LIGHT OF THE WORLD.

BEHOLD me standing at the door,
 And hear me asking o'er and o'er,
With pleading voice above the din,
 " May I come in ?   May I come in ? "

Wearing the cruel thorns for thee,
I listen long and patiently,
To hear the footstep from within,
 " May I come in ?   May I come in ? "

I fought for thee with Death's grim wave ;
I burst his dungeons of the grave ;
I would my rightful guerdon win,
 " May I come in ?   May I come in ? "

Ye dream dark dreams alone by night,
And lo, I am the Living Light,
That smiles away all mists of sin.
   " May I come in ?   May I come in ? "

There's surely room upon thy breast
For one more loving head to rest :
One empty place for kith and kin.
   " May I come in ?   May I come in ? "

I would not have thee beat in vain
Our Father's door and plead in pain,
When Heaven and all its joys begin.
   " May I come in ?   May I come in ? "

GOING TO SCHOOL.

ON Sunday morning early,
　　While yet the grass is pearly,
　The air is bright and cool;
All clad in our best graces,
With rosy morning faces,
　　We go to the Sunday School!

To-day is Life in blossom:
Heartsease in every bosom,
　And all is beautiful.
A spirit within us springing
At Heaven's gate will be singing
　　Thanks for the Sunday School!

We sun us in its brightness;
We clothe us in its whiteness,
  As doth the wayside pool,
That holds from Morn till Even,
Its little bit of Heaven—
  The gladsome Sunday School !

Here learn we how to lighten
The heaviest lot, and brighten
  The day most dark with dool,
And lay up Childhood's treasure,
To reap immortal pleasure
  Even in a Sunday School !

The summer Earth rejoices,
With hers we lift our voices,
  And Heaven blends the whole.
And when God's Angels cover us,
Drawing the darkness over us,
  They bless the Sunday School !

PARENTS' PRAYER FOR THE
CHILDREN.

CHRIST on Earth, in Heaven the King,
  As we heard the Children sing,
How the thought within us smiled,
Thou wert once a little Child !

Hover near them, Heavenly Dove,
With thine overshadowing love ;
Keep them pure and undefiled :
Thou wert once a little Child !

See them playing on the sands,
'Twixt two tides, with helpless hands ;
Save them when the waves grow wild :
Thou wert once a little Child !

Bless them in their joyousness;
Hear them, help them, in distress;
Be their Shepherd when beguiled;
Thou wert once a little Child!

Let their feet be firmly shod;
Let them not go back to God,
With immortal jewels soiled;
Thou wert once a little Child!

Take them, when the Peril's past,
To thy Father's Home at last;
He remembers, and is mild,
Thou wert once a little Child!

CHILDREN'S EVENING PRAYER.

GRACIOUS Saviour ! meekly crave your
    Little Lambs their fold to-night ;
Do Thou hear us, and be near us ;
    Thro' the darkness lead to light :
    Fence our weakness with Thy might !

Night is nearing ! timid, fearing
    Life is shrinking in its nest ;
To Thy keeping take us sleeping,
    Gentle Shepherd, in Thy breast,
    Where we nestle and are blest !

Thro' the nightfall may Thy Light fall
  On us, safely hid apart,
When no change or passing danger
  Clouds us, with Thy smile at heart.
  Where the lambs are there Thou art !

White mists wreathing their soft breathing,
  Where the water-courses run,
From their hiding-place are gliding,
  Hanging dew-drops one by one,
  To be lighted by the sun !

We too kneeling for Thy healing,
  Pray Thy dews may fall apace
In rich showers, that Thy Flowers
  May uplift their morning face,
  Glistening with Thy freshest grace.

May good Angels with evangels
  Glad our slumbers by one gleam
Of their covering white wings, hovering
  Down the ladder of our dream—
  Soft the hardest pillow will seem !

O Thou Solace of the weary;
O Thou Rest for all that roam;
Nightless Sunshine for the dreary;
For the Homeless endless home;
To Thy waiting arms we come!

AND THEY SUNG A NEW SONG.

HEAR what the Saint in solemn dream was
    shown
  Thro' Heaven's own Gates of Gold ;
He saw them standing by the great White Throne ;
  He heard their raptures roll'd !
Christ was the Sun of that new firmament,
  And there was no more night,
While thro' the golden City harping went
  The glorious all in white.

These, out of their great tribulation, came
  To bow before the Throne !
These lifted up their foreheads from the flame
  And by His name were known !

Some on the rack were living witnesses,
    And many fell a-field ;
But Christ did greet His Martyrs with a kiss,
    And all their hurts were heal'd.

These had to wrestle with wild waves of strife,
    Long ere they reach'd that shore
Where they at last have won the crowns of life
    They wear for evermore.
There do they drink of Life's all-healing Stream,
    And quench their thirst of years ;
All star-like now the precious jewels gleam,
    They sow'd on Earth as tears.

Help us, O Lord, to reach that Better Land,
    Afar from sorrow and sin,
And join that Blessed band all harp-in-hand,
    All safe with Christ shut in.
Feeble and poor the songs we sing ! at most,
    Some selfish Prayer we raise ;
While the white Harpers on that Heavenly coast,
    Hymn everlasting Praise.

THE ASPEN.

I WENT out into the wistful night,
   Along with my little Daughter ;
Down in the valley the weird Moonlight
   With an Elfin shine lit the wan water.

The Trees stood dark in a flame of white ;
   A Nightingale sang in the stillness ;
It seemed the husht heart of the sweet spring
      night
   Brimmed over because of its fulness.

Not a breath of air in the region wide ;
   Not a ripple upon the river ;
Yet all of a sudden the Aspens sigh'd
   And thro' all their leaves ran a shiver.

My darling she nestled quite close to me
 For such shield as mine arms could give her;
" *There went not the least waft of wind thro' the*
  Tree;
 Then why did the Aspens shiver ? "

I told her the tale, how, by Kedron's Brook
 Our Saviour one evening wander'd;
A cloud came over His glorified look
 As he paused by the way and ponder'd.

The trees felt his sighing; their heads all bow'd
 Towards Him in solemn devotion,
Save the Aspen, that stood up so stately and proud;
 It made neither murmur nor motion.

Then the Holy One lifted His face of pain :
 " *The Aspen shall quake and shiver,*
From this time forth till I come again,
 Whether growing by Brook or by River."

And oft in the listening hush of night
 The Aspen will secretly shiver;
With all its tremulous leaves turn white,
 Like a guilty thing by the River.

So the souls that look on His sorrow and pain
    For their sake, and bow not, may quiver
Like Aspens, and quake when He comes again,
    Thro' the night for ever, for ever !

POOR ELLEN.

'TIS hard to *die* in Spring-time,
    When, to mock our bitter need,
All life around runs over
    In its fulness without heed :
New life for tiniest twig on tree,
New worlds of honey for the bee,
And not one drop of dew for me
    Who perish as I plead.

'Tis *hard* to die in Spring-time,
    When it stirs the poorest clod ;
The wee Wren lifts its little heart
    In lusty songs to God ;

s

And Summer comes with conquering march ;
Her banners waving 'neath the arch
Of heaven, where I lie and parch—
 Left dying by the road.

'*Tis* hard to die in Spring-time,
 When the long blue days unfold,
And cowslip-coloured sunsets
 Grow, like Heaven's own heart, pure gold !
Each breath of balm brings wave on wave
Of new life that would lift and lave
My Life, whose *feel* is of the grave,
 And mingling with the mould.

But sweet to die in Spring-time,
 When these lustres of the sward,
And all the breaks of beauty
 Wherewith Earth is daily starr'd,
For me are but the outside show,
All leading to the inner glow
Of that strange world to which I go—
 For ever with the Lord.

O sweet to die in Spring-time,
 When I reach the promised Rest,

And feel His arm is round me—
    Know I sink back on His breast :
His kisses close these poor dim eyes ;
Soon I shall hear Him say " Arise,"
And, springing up with glad surprise,
    Shall know Him and be blest.

'Tis sweet to die in Spring-time,
    For I feel my golden year
Of summer-time eternal
    Is beginning even here !
" Poor Ellen ! " now you say and sigh,
" Poor Ellen ! " and to-morrow I
Shall say " Poor Mother ! " and, from the sky,
    Watch *you*, and wait you there.

THE SUNKEN CITY.

BY day it lies hidden and lurks beneath
    The ripples that laugh with light :
But calmly and clearly and coldly as death,
    It glooms into shape by night,
When none but the awful Heavens and me
Can look on the City that's sunk in the sea.

Many a Castle I built in the air ;
    Towers that gleamed in the sun ;
Spires that soared so stately and fair
    They toucht heaven every one,
Lie under the waters that mournfully
Closed over the City that's sunk in the sea.

Many fine houses, but never a home ;
   Windows, and no live face !
Doors set wide where no beating hearts come ;
   No voice is heard in the place :
It sleeps in the arms of Eternity—
The silent City that's sunk in the sea.

There the face of a dead love lies,
   Embalmed in the bitterest tears ;
No breath on the lips ! no smile in the eyes,
   Tho' you watcht for years and years :
And the dear drowned eyes never close from me,
Looking up from the City that's sunk in the sea.

Two of the bonniest birds of God
   That ever warmed human heart
For a nest, till they fluttered their wings abroad,
   Lie in their chambers apart—
Dead ! yet pleading piteously
In the lonesome City that's sunk in the sea.

O ! the brave ventures there lying in wreck,
   Dark on that shore o' the Lost !

Gone down, with every hope on deck,
  When all-sail for a glorious coast !
And the waves go sparkling splendidly
Over the City that's sunk in the sea.

Then I look from my City that's sunk in the sea
  To that Star-Chamber overhead ;
And torturingly they question me—
  " *What of this world of the dead*
That lies out of sight, and how will it be
With the City and thee, when there's no more sea ? "

THE LIFE BEYOND.

ALTHOUGH its features fade in light of unimagined bliss,
We have shadowy revealings of the Better World in
this.

A little glimpse, when Spring unveils her face and
opes her eyes,
Of the Sleeping Beauty in the soul that wakes in
Paradise.

A little drop of Heaven in each diamond of the
shower,
A breath of the Eternal in the fragrance of each
flower !

A little low vibration in the warble of Night's
    bird,
Of the praises and the music that shall be hereafter
    heard !

A little whisper in the leaves that clap their hands
    and try
To glad the heart of man, and lift to Heaven his
    thankful eye !

A little semblance mirror'd in old Ocean's smile or
    frown
Of His vast glory who doth bow the Heavens and
    come down !

A little symbol shining through the worlds that
    move at rest
On invisible foundations of the broad almighty
    breast !

A little hint that stirs and thrills the wings we
    fold within,
And tells of that full heaven *yonder* which must
    here begin !

A little springlet welling from the fountain-head
    above,
That takes its earthly way to find the ocean of all
    love !

A little silver shiver in the ripple of the river
Caught from the light that knows no night for ever
    and for ever !

A little hidden likeness, often faded and defiled,
Of the great, the good All-father, in His poorest
    human child !

Although the best be lost in light of unimagined
    bliss,
We have shadowy revealings of the Better World
    in this.

IN A DREAM.

SHE came but for a little while,
    Yet with a wondrous gleam !
She left within my soul her smile,
    The Darling of my Dream !

O face too clear for sorrow or tear,
    Too real for masks that seem ;
I seek, but shall not find you Here,
    You Darling of my Dream !

I wonder do you wait for me
    Beside the glad Life-Stream,
Or under the Leaf-of-Healing tree—
    You Darling of my Dream ?

O sometimes lift your veil by night,
And let one beauty-beam
Fill all my life for days with light,
You Darling of my Dream !

A CRY IN THE NIGHT.

DARK, dark the night, and tearfully I grope,
    Lost in the Shadows, feeling for the way,
But cannot find it.   Here's no help, no hope,
    And God is very far off with His day.

Hush, hush, faint heart ! why this may be thy
        chance,
    When all is at the worst, to prove thy faith ;
Stand still, and see His great Deliverance,
    And trust Him at the darkest unto death.

Often upon the last grim ridge of war
    God takes His stand to aid us in the fight ;
He watches while we roll the tide afar,
    And, beaten back, is near us with His might.

We hear the Arrows in the dark go by:
  The cowering soul no longer soars or sings,
Or it might know His presence then most nigh,
  Our darkness being the Shadow of His wings.

No need of faith if all were visibly clear!
  'Tis for the trial-time its help was given;
Tho' clouds be thick, the Sun is just as near
  That shines within and makes the heart its
    heaven.

Amidst our wildest night of saddest woes,
  When Earth is desolate—Heaven dark with
    doom,
Faith has its fire-flash of the soul that shows
  The face of the Eternal thro' the gloom.

A SONG IN THE MORNING.

AWAKE, poor Soul, the Shadows flee,
  Dawn kindles in the sky,
Lift up the drooping head, and see
  Redemption draweth nigh !

A little further we must bear
  The load, and do our best ;
Then take immortal solace where
  The Weary are at rest.

A few more Meetings on the Deep,
  And partings on the shore ;
And then in Heaven at last we keep
  Our tryst for evermore.

And we shall see the lifted head
 Once bowed to show His face ;
And feel the arms in death He spread,
 Close round us in embrace !

The Devil, standing in our light,
 And darkening all our day,
Shall wave his wings for final flight ;
 His shadow pass away.

Our Pilgrimage will soon be past,
 Our worst afflictions borne ;
Some weary Night, 'twill be our last,
 And then Eternal Morn.

HIS BANNER OVER ME.

SURROUNDED by unnumber'd Foes,
    Against my soul the battle goes !
Yet tho' I weary, sore distress'd,
I know that I shall reach my Rest :
    I lift my tearful eyes above,—
    His Banner over me is Love.

Its Sword my spirit will not yield,
Tho' flesh may faint upon the field ;
He waves before my fading sight
The branch of palm—the crown of light ;
    I lift my brightening eyes above,—
    His Banner over me is Love.

My cloud of battle-dust may dim ;
His veil of splendour curtain Him !
And in the midnight of my fear
I may not feel Him standing near :
    But, as I lift mine eyes above,
    His Banner over me is Love.

THE TWO HEAVENS.

THERE are two Heavens for natures clear
  And calm as thine, my gentle Love!
One Heaven but reflected here;
  One Heaven that waits above:

As yonder Lake, in Evening's red,
  Lies smiling with the smile of Rest:
One Heaven glowing overhead;
  One mirror'd in its breast.

HOW IT SEEMS.

STARS in the Midnight's blue abyss
So closely shine they seem to kiss;
But, Darling, they are far apart;
They close not beating heart to heart:

And high in glory many a Star
Glows, lighting other worlds afar,
Whilst hiding in its breast the dearth
And darkness of a fireless hearth.

All happy to the listener seems
The Singer, with his gracious gleams;
His music rings, his ardours glow
Divinely; Ah, we know, we know!

For all the beauty he sheds, we see
How bare his own poor life may be ;
He gives ambrosia, wanting bread ;
Makes balm for Hearts, with ache of head.

He finds the Laurel budding yet,
From Love transfigured and tear-wet ;
They are his life-drops turned to Flowers
That make so sweet this world of ours !

ALBERT THE GOOD.

ALBERT THE GOOD.

SOME two-and-twenty golden years ago,
 A noble Wooer to our England came ;
To-day, he has won her, lying pale and low.
 Albert the Good we write his royal name.

The Power that sits enthroned by open graves
 Hath risen to rule the air. His death-bell tolls,
And rolls upon us in dull heavy waves,
 Sepulchral shadows over living souls.

On every burdened wind the sound is borne,
 Invisibly swift the sparks electric slide ;
Till, under archways of full many a morn,
 The gloom of our great loss will visibly glide.

The meanest doorway darkens at this cloud,
   The poorest poor have lost a personal friend ;
Down to one level are the loftiest bowed ;
   In the large clasp of nature all hearts blend.

The gush of gladness in our eyes is dimmed ;
   Christmas hath lost its glow of merry heart-shine ;
The Wassail-cup will pass as tho' 'twere brimmed
   With the red, solemn, sacramental wine,

And dark in His extinguished light we stand.
   In every face we read how much bereft !
A sterner pressure of the grasping hand
   Tells of our loss, and clings to what is left.

For he was one of those we never know
   Till they have left us, nor how great the love
We bore them ; they are all too meek to show
   Their dearness, till they stand our praise above.

How should we mirror truly when a breath
   Set all the surface in a blurring strife ?
We are calmer now !—touched by the hand of
    Death !—
   To hold the lustrous image of his life.

We met him coldly, and on looking back
  See all our dimness by his kindling glow.
The mist we breathed hath served to mark his track
  And make a starrier halo for his brow.

At last our clouds of earth are cleared away !
  Albert the Good goes patiently to God ;
Smiling back to us with his frank blue day,
  He leaves us shining footprints where he trod.

We know that when our mortal work is done,
  Few to the Master's keeping will return
A fairer copy of the life His Son
  Once left us, or a warmer " well done " earn.

Down goes the scaffolding, the work is crown'd ;
  Much that was hidden from us may be read,
And for the first time we can look all round
  The Statue of his life now perfected.

The Flower of Chivalry upon the height,
  As featly could he bend to lowliest place ;
With something in his presence of the light
  That sweetly shone in Philip Sidney's face.

He held for ever hallowed the dear breasts
   Where nestling Love and its sweet babes had
     lain ;
For ever sacred kept Home's secret nest
   Of purest pleasure and of proudest pain.

His natural kingliness made crowns look wan,
   Whom God had set amongst the Lords of Earth,
To show them how the majesty of Man
   May shine above the starriest badge of Birth.

A calm, high life, crown'd with a quiet death !
   His robe of pain around him folding, he
Was not the man to waste his dying breath ;
   Who nobly lives, can die with dignity.

The gentle spirit did not wish to hear
   The women moaning thro' the house for him,
But only sought to feel its darlings near
   Enough to bless them when 'twas getting dim !

No need of courtly lies for comforting ;
   For he can face the truth, tho' stern and wild :
Thro' spiritual rehearsal, he can wring
   The victory ! and his soul within him smiled.

And 'tis not near so hard for one to bow
  And enter the dark doorway of the Tomb,
Who has learnt to meet Death kneeling with
    bent brow;
  Whose inner light can pierce that inner gloom.

And while in sorrow here we dimly sit,
  We lift the head, to ease an aching breast,
And, looking up, behold the Stars are lit;
  And there's another in the realms of Rest.

Rest, happy soul, in thy salvation deep;
  The top of life, and endless day for thee;
While in the valleys here we sit and weep
  Among the shadows of Eternity.

We can but kneel, and grope, and kiss His feet
  Who takes thee to His infinite embrace;
We feel transfigured if our touch may meet
  His garment's hem; but *thou* behold'st His face.

Poor widowed Queen! we see her as she trod
  The Aisle where Music's mellow thunders rolled,
And Heaven opened, and the smile of God
  In sunbeams crown'd her head with saintly gold.

And how we listened—knowing she was blest—
   To the proud murmurs of the brooding dove ;
Home-pleasures round the royal Mother pressed,
   And God gave many voices to her love.

And now the cloud of this calamity
   Darkens the crown we set on her young brow :
Ah, look up to the side next Heaven, and see
   'Tis God Himself that crowns our lady now !

With all hearts aching for the folded face,
   We can but grasp His hand in prayer for her !
So lonely in her desolate, high place ;
   And leave her with the Eternal Comforter.

Though two be parted in that shadow drear,
   Where one must walk alone, yet is it given
For the dear blessëd spirit to be near ;
   The human vision with the voice in Heaven.

It is my faith they friend us in our need ;
   With tender chords they draw us where they
     move ;
And often at the noon of night they feed
   With dews of Heaven the lilies of their love.

Warm whispers will come stealing like a glow
    Of God, to kiss the spirit's sealëd eyes
Till they be opened, and true love doth know
    Its Marriage Garden blooms in Paradise.

Here hearts may beat so close that two lives make
    Only one shadow in the sun we see,
But, in the light we see not, these shall wake
    One angel—wedded for eternity.

The sap is swarth and bitter in the bark,
    That sweetens in the sunny fruit above,
And spirits yearning upward thro' the dark
    Shall reach and summer in their light of love.

This mourning shall be made majestic mirth ;
    This grief shall be a glory otherwhere ;
The music that we hear no more on earth
    Will help to make up Heaven when we are there.

And Thou, young Prince, whose Pilot saw thee tide
    Safe o'er the reefs beyond the harbour-bar,
Then left thee—beaconing o'er the waters wide,
    This Star of Morn shall rise, thine Evening Star.

May thy life flourish, ripen hour by hour,
   And heavenward draw the virtues of thy root;
Our eyes have seen the beauty of the flower,
   Do thou unfold the glory of the fruit.

We build his Monument, but men may see
   His steady lustre live in thee and thine;
And thou mayest bear, to Empires yet to be,
   The goodness and the glory of thy line.

Think of the dear face dark beneath the mould,
   And be thou to us what he would have been;
So shall the secret springs of sorrows old
   Give to thy future paths a gladder green.

This is a waiting hour of wonder for
   A world; our England looks across her waves!
Will the Dove seek her bosom, or red War,
   Whose footprints tread deep pits for gory
      graves?

Is it the kiss of Peace and Righteousness,
   That softly thrills the husht, grim silence through,
Or Battle's bugle-cry that makes us press
   All sail—send up our brave old bit of blue?

We know not.   But, if foot to foot we stand,
  On slippery boarding-plank, or ruddied sward,
'Twill be the sturdier stroke for our dear Land
  That holds another grave like this to guard.

And all is well that makes a People one,
  Even   though   the   meeting - place   be   Albert's
    tomb :
We gather grapes of joy up in the sun,
  But our best wine must ripen in the gloom.

Many true hearts have mouldered down to enrich
  The roots of England's greatness underground ;
Until, below, as wide and strong they stretch,
  As overhead the branches reach around.

And so our England's glory ever grows,
  And so her stature rises ever higher,
Until the faces of her farthest foes
  Darken with envy, overshadowed by her.

So climb the heavens, Old Tree, until the gold
  Stars glisten as thy fruitage—heave thy breast
And broaden till the fiercest storms shall fold
  Their wings within thy shelter and find rest.

COUSIN WINNIE.

U

COUSIN WINNIE.

THE glad spring-green grows luminous,
    With coming Summer's golden glow ;
Merry Birds sing as they sang to us
    In far-off seasons, long ago :
The old place brings the young Dawn back,
    That moist eyes mirage in their dew ;
My heart goes forth along the track
    Where oft it danced, dear Winnie, with you.
A world of Time, a sea of change,
    Have rolled between the paths we tread,
Since you were my " *Cousin Winnie*," and I
    Was your " *own little, good little Ned.*"

There's where I nearly broke my neck,
   Climbing for nests ! and hid my pain :
And then I thought your heart would break,
   To have the Birds put back again.
Yonder, with lordliest tenderness,
   I carried you across the Brook ;
So happy in my arms to press
   You, triumphing in your timid look :
So lovingly you leaned to mine
   Your cheek of sweet and dusky red :
You were my " *Cousin Winnie,*" and I
   Was your " *own little, good little Ned.*"

My Being in your presence bask'd,
   And kitten-like for pleasure purr'd ;
A higher heaven I never ask'd,
   Than watching, wistful as a bird,
To hear that voice so rich and low ;
   Or sun me in the rosy rise
Of some soul-ripening smile, and know
   The thrill of opening paradise.
The Boy might look too tenderly,
   All lightly 'twas interpreted :
You were my " *Cousin Winnie,*" and I
   Was your " *own little, good little Ned.*"

Ay me, but I remember how
   I felt the heart-break, bitterly,
When the Well-handle smote your brow,
   Because the blow fell not on me !
Such holy longing fill'd my life,
   I could have died, Dear, for your sake ;
But, never thought of you as Wife ;
   A cure to clasp for love's heart-ache.
You enter'd my soul's temple, Dear,
   Something to worship, not to wed :
You were my " *Cousin Winnie*," and I
   Was your " *own little, good little Ned.*"

I saw you, heaven on heaven higher,
   Grow into stately womanhood ;
Your beauty kindling with the fire
   That swims in proud old English blood.
Away from me,—a radiant Joy !
   You soar'd ; fit for a Hero's bride :
While I a Man in soul, a Boy
   In stature, shiver'd at your side !
You saw not how the poor wee Love
   Pined dumbly, and thus doubly pled :
You were my " *Cousin Winnie*," and I
   Was your " *own little, good little Ned.*"

And then that other voice came in !
    There my Life's music suddenly stopp'd.
Silence and darkness fell between
    Us, and my Star from heaven dropp'd.
I led Him by the hand to you—
    He was my Friend—whose name you bear :
I had prayed for some great task to do,
    To prove my love.   I did it, Dear !
He was not jealous of poor me ;
    Nor saw my life bleed under his tread :
You were my " *Cousin Winnie,*" and I
    Was your " *own little, good little Ned.*"

I smiled, Dear, at your happiness—
    So Martyrs smile upon the spears—
The smile of your reflected bliss
    Flasht from my heart's dark tarn of tears !
In love, that made the suffering sweet,
    My blessing with the rest was given—
" *God's softest flowers kiss her feet*
    On Earth, and crown Her head in Heaven."
And lest the heart should leap to tell
    Its tale i' the eyes, I bow'd the head :
You were my " *Cousin Winnie,*" and I
    Was your " *own little, good little Ned.*"

I do not blame you, Darling mine ;
   You could not know the love that lurkt
To make my life so intertwine
   With yours, and with mute mystery workt.
And, had you known, how distantly
   Your calm eyes would have lookt it down,
Darkling with all the majesty
   Of Midnight wearing her star-crown !
Into its virgin veil of cloud,
   The startled dearness would have fled.
You were my " *Cousin Winnie*," and 1
   Was your " *own little, good little Ned.*"

I stretch my hand across the years ;
   Feel, Dear, the heart still pulses true :
I have often dropp'd internal tears,
   Thinking the kindest thoughts of you.
I have fought like one in iron, they said,
   Who through the battle follow'd me.
I struck the blows for you, and bled
   Within my armour secretly.
Not caring for the cheers, my heart
   Far into the golden time had fled :
You were my " *Cousin Winnie*," and I
   Was your " *own little, good little Ned.*"

I sometimes see you in my dreams,
    Asking for aid I may not give :
Down from your eyes the sorrow streams,
    And helplessly I look and grieve
At arms that toss with wild heartache,
    And secrets writhing to be told :
I start to hear your voice, and wake.
    There's nothing but the moaning cold !
Sometimes I pillow in mine arms
    The darling little rosy head.
You are my " *Cousin Winnie*," and I
    Am your " *own little, good little Ned.*"

I wear the name of Hero now,
    And flowers at my feet are cast ;
I feel the crown about my brow—
    So keen the thorns that hold it fast !
Ay me, and I would rather wear
    The cooling green and luminous glow
Of one you made with Cowslips, Dear,
    A many golden Springs ago.
Your gentle fingers did not give
    This ache of heart, this throb of head,
When you were my " *Cousin Winnie*," and I
    Was your " *own little, good little Ned.*"

Unwearying, lonely, year by year,
   I go on laying up my love.
I think God makes no promise here
   But it shall be fulfilled above;
I think my wild weed of the waste
   Will one day prove a flower most sweet;
My love shall bear its fruit at last—
   'Twill all be righted when we meet;
And I shall find them gather'd up
   In pearls for you—the tears I've shed
Since you were my " *Cousin Winnie*," and I
   Was your " *own little, good little Ned.*"

A WINTER'S TALE FOR THE LITTLE ONES.

A WINTER'S TALE FOR THE LITTLE ONES.

A MERRY sound of clapping hands,
    A call to see the sight ;
And lo ! the first soft snow-flakes fall,
So exquisitely virginal.
'Tis my wee Nell at window stands,
    And the world is all in white.

Her eyes, where dawns my bluest Day,
    Dance with the dancing snow !
I see delicious shivers thrill
Her thro' and thro'. She feels the chill
Of Earth so white, and skies so grey
    Enrich our fireside glow.

" *No Winters now, my little Maid,*
    Like those that used to come,
Making our Christmas sparkle, bright
As crystallised plum-cake at night,
And Frost his Puck-like trickeries played,
    With fancies frolicsome.

" *He fix'd your breath in flowers, the Trees*
    To Chandeliers would turn :
He pincht your toes, he nipped your nose,
And made your cheek a wrinkled Rose :
Perhaps at night you heard him sneeze,
    And the Jug was crackt at morn !

" *The Snow-Storms were magnificent !*
    And in the clear, still weather,
Against the bitter wintry blue,
And Sunset's orange-tawny hue,
You saw the smoke straight upward went,
    For weeks and weeks together.

" *At night the Waits mixt with our dream*
    Their music sweet and low :

We children knew not as we heard,
Each, listening, nestled like a Bird,
Whether from Heaven the music came.
    Or only over the snow !

" *No winters now-a-days like those.*"
    And then my darling tries
To coax me for a " *tale that's true :*
A story that is new—quite new."
And up the arch of wonder goes,
    Above the frank, blue eyes !

" *Once on a time*"—" *Do tell me when,*
    And where ?" says my wee Nell—
" *When Christmas came on Thursday—now,*
Some five-and-thirty years ago !
Superbly we were snowed-up then,
    Who lived in Ingle Dell.

" *His icy Drawbridge Winter dropped ;*
    The running springs he froze ;
The Roads were lost ; the hedges crossed ;
All field-work ceased through the ' Long Frost.'
But there was one thing never stopped—
    That was Grandmother's nose !

" *The snow might fall by day, by night,*
   The weather grow more rough,
And up to our bedroom windows heap
The drift, and smother men like sheep,
And wrap the world in a shroud of white—
   Old Gran must have her snuff!

" *So, Uncle Willie, then a lad*
   Not more than nine years old,
Upon the Christmas morn must go
And fetch her snuff, and face the Snow,
Which surely had gone dancing mad,
   And wrestle with the cold.

" *Wrapt in his crimson Comforter,*
   His basket on his arm,
He started.   Mother follow'd him
With her proud eyes so dewy-dim ;
While kisses from the heart of her
   Within his heart were warm.

" *How gentle is the gracious Snow,*
   When first you watch her dance ;

Her feathery flutter, winding whorls ;
Her finish perfect as the pearl's ;
She looks you in the face as tho'
   'Twere unveil'd Innocence.

" But now, 'tis wild upon the waste,
   And wing'd upon the wind :
You see, just passing out of sight,
The Ghost of things in a swirl of white !—
The Storm unwinkingly he faced,
   Tho' it snow'd enough to blind.

" Fire-pointed, stinging, strikes and burns
   To the bone, each icy dart.
He stumbles—falls—is up again,
And onward for the Town a-strain ;
Backward our Willie never turns,
   And never loses heart.

" He looks a weird and wintry Elf
   With face in ruddy glow ;
And all his curls are straighten'd out,
Hanging in Icicles about
A sparkling statue of himself,
   Shaped out of frozen snow.

X

" *He still fought on, for tho' the Storm*
    Might bend him, he was tough ;
And when the Blast would take his breath,
With kisses like the kiss of death,
One thought still kept his courage warm—
    It was Grandmother's Snuff !

" *At length with many a danger pass'd,*
    Unboding any to come,
He has got the Snuff.   Far more than food,
Or wine, 'twill warm her poor old blood.
He has it safe at last, at last !
    And sets his face for Home.

" *He has the Snuff; but it were well*
    If Granny had it too !
For early closes such a day,
And wild and dreary is the way ;
If dark before he reach the Dell,
    What can poor Willie do ?

" *Within the Town the blast is husht ;*
    The snow-flakes from you melt :

But out upon the pathless moor,
The storm grows wilder than before ;
And at him all its furies rusht,
   Till he faint and fainter felt.

" His thoughts are whirling with the Snow :
   His eyes wax dizzy and dim !
And on the path, 'twixt him and night,
Now dancing left, now dancing right,
It seems a white Witch-Woman doth go,
   With white hand beckoning him !

" To the last stile he clung—maybe
   A furlong from our door ;
Then miss'd his footing on the plank,
And deep into the snow-drift sank.
O, my belovëd Willie, we
   Shall never see you more !

" Ah, they lookt long and wistfully
   Who waiting sat at home :
They strained their eyes thro' the deepening dark,
At every sound they lean'd to hark ;
And wonder'd where could Willie be,
   And when would Willie come ?

" *Thro' all that night of wild affright*
  They search'd the road to Town ;
They called him high, they call'd him low,
They mock'd each other thro' the snow,
And all the night, by lanthorn light,
  They wander'd up and down.

" *They sought him where the waters plash*
  Darkly by Deadman's Cave !
They sought him at the Rag-Pit, near
The Mill, and by the lonesome Weir ;
At the Cross-Roads where ' Harry's Ash '
  Grows from the Suicide's Grave.

" *In Ingle Dell they locked no door,*
  Put out no light.   At such
A time you cling to a little thing
That's done for neighbourly comforting !
Old Gran thought she'd take snuff no more,
  And she took thrice as much.

" *All night the Snow with fingers soft*
  Kept pointing to the ground.

Only too well they knew 'twas there;
But had no hint to guide them where!
And he so near. They passed him oft,
  Close by his white grave-mound."

" And did he die?" cries little Nell.
  " No, he was nestled warm.
It seemed the white arm round him curled
And caught him in another world :
What other world he could not tell,
  But, out of all the storm.

" And all was chang'd too suddenly
  For him to know the place.
He swooned awhile, and when he woke
A lightning from his darkness broke.
Alone with the Eternal he
  Was standing face to face!

" There in his grave alive, he knew
  He stood, or sat upright!
With burning brain, and freezing feet.
And he so young, and life so sweet!
And, bitter thought! what would Gran do
  Without her snuff that night?

" *A long, long night of sixty hours*
 Did Willie pass. I know
Not how he lived. But Heaven can hold
A life as safe as Earth can fold
Her hidden life of fruit and flowers,
 Thro' her long trance of snow.

" ' *Tis Sabbath day. How quietly gleams*
 That Snow-drift o'er him driven !
The winds are softly laid asleep,
In their white snow-bed covered deep.
The white Clouds all so still ! it seems
 Like Sunday up in Heaven

" *The Country-folk are passing near*
 His tomb—no tale it tells—
Old Ploughmen in their white smockfrocks,
Old Women in long scarlet cloaks,
And Lad and Lass,—when on his ear
 There faints a sound of Bells

" *And, looking up, a tiny hole*
 Was melted with his breath ;

Wherethro' a bit of God's blue sky
Was smiling on him like an Eye;
A living eye with a loving soul
   Shone in that face of death!

"O joy! He shouted from his grave,
   And finding room to stir,
He tooth and nail began to climb;
He clutcht the top o' the bank this time;
Thrust his hand thro' the snow to wave
   His good old Comforter!

" 'I'm here!' 'It's me!' His flag they see,
   And know lost Willie's voice;
They quickly answer shout for shout,
And with their hands they dig him out,
And carry him home. O! didn't we
   In Ingle Dell rejoice?

" There be some tears that smile, and such
   Were wept by Woman and Man.
But while they glistened in each eye,
He pulled the snuff out sound and dry;
Snow might cover him, cold might clutch,
   The Snuff was safe for Gran."

WILLIAM MAKEPEACE THACKERAY.

WILLIAM MAKEPEACE THACKERAY.

THE Merry Bells ring in the Christmas Day,
    While in our hearts a mournful knell is
        knoll'd,
    As other tidings thro' the land are roll'd—
Telling of a great spirit pass'd away.

Another heart of English Oak gone down,
    Like some three-decker striking with no word
    Of warning ; sails all set ; all hands aboard ;
When sunniest skies are smiling with their crown.

Low lies the stately form that tower'd so tall,
    With life so lusty, and with look so brave ;
    The head thrown back, as if to breast the wave
For many a year—the wave that whelmeth all.

For all the sobs that rise, or tears that rain,
 No more fond, fatherly words for Lad and Lass !
 No more across his manly face will pass
The light of passion, or the shadow of pain.

We never told our love !   He would have thought
 We prattled prettily, amused the while ;
 And held us at a distance with his smile,
Until we hid the presents we had brought.

Now we might stroke the almost young, white hair,
 And even kiss the cold and quiet brow ;
 The heart may have its way, and speak out now !
He will not mock us, lying silent there !

A nature—not at first sight meant to win—
 That prickly for protection grows without,
 To safely fence its tenderness about,
And fold the sweet virginities within :

Just as you find a nest whose outer form
 Looks grimly rugged when the boughs are bare ;
 The birds have flown—you peep inside, and there
How softly it is lined ! how brooding-warm !

He had our English way of making fun
   Of those shy feelings which our hearts will hold
   Like dew-drops all a-tremble, and enfold
Them with our strength—sacred from storm and
   sun.

We listen'd to his voice, as some true Wife,
   Upon her Husband's breast may lean her head,
   While many things in her dispraise are said
By Him ; but, she leans closer, life to life,

For, while the covert words sound on above,
   Their other, deeper meaning she divines ;
   She hears the heart ; knows its masonic signs ;
And nestles in a bosom large with love.

So loud he cried, a Snake in Beauty's bower ;
   A Worm that gnaws at life's most human root ;
   A Wasp that revels in our rarest fruit ;
So gently breathed the fragrance of the flower !

He kept his Show-Box—scant of Mirrors where
   You saw Eternity whose worlds we pass
   Darkly by daylight, but, with many a glass,
Reflecting all the Humours of the Fair !

The thousand shapes of vanity and sin ;
  Toy-stalls of Satan ; the mad masquerade :
  The floating Pleasures that before them play'd :
The foolish faces following, all a-grin.

He slily prickt the bubbles that we blew ;
  He cheer'd us on to chase our thistle-down ;
  Crowning the winner with a fool's-cap crown ;
And *Bon-Bons* mottoed in quaint mockery threw.

Then in the merry midst some sad, strange words
  Would touch the spring of tears.   His eyes were
      dry,
  And, as your laughters ceased, were wondering
      why ?
Laugh on !   He had only struck the minor
    chords !

He was not one of those who are light at heart
  Because 'tis empty in its airy swing :
  He found the world too full of sorrowing,
But, show'd us how to smile and bear our
    smart.

Many of God's most precious gifts are sad
　　To tears, and, tho' no weeper, this he knew.
　　So, in our merry wine, would steep the rue,
That with a manlier strength we might grow glad.

And, year by year, still kindlier to the last,
　　He drew us towards him ; showing more and
　　　　more,
　　The heart of honey, human to the core,
That into Love's full flower ripened fast :

Thus Music sweetens to the latest breath,
　　And closer draws the leaning, listening ear ;
　　And still it whispers, from its heaven near,
Of some more perfect sweetness beyond death.

Large-hearted, brave, sincere, compassionate !
　　We could not guess one-half the Angels see :
　　They found you out, Old Friend, ere we did ! We
But reach the nobler justice all too late.

Soft, O Belovëd ! be your early Rest,
　　And sweet its quiet where the grassy green
　　Shuts out so many and many a sorry scene :
Heaven sun the hoarded fragrance from your breast !

And may the Spirit that with us but gropes
    And stirs our earth, and yearns up thro' our
        night
    In strivings dumb, with you have found the
        Light
That giveth eyes to poor, blind human hopes.

For us—I know you would have us put away
    The tears ; draw closer, fill the gap, and keep
    Old kindly customs ; sing the sorrow asleep,
And all make merry, this being Christ's own day.

A ROYAL WEDDING CHIME.

Y

A ROYAL WEDDING CHIME.

M ANY a time, from out the North,
   The fire-eyed Raven flew,
And England watcht its sailing forth,
   With eyes of wistful blue;
Many a time her True-hearts stood
   All ranked and ready for
Grim welcome, should the Bird of Blood
   Swoop down on wings of war!

To-day, another Norland Bird
   Comes floating o'er the foam;
And England's heart of hearts is stirred
   To have the dear bird Home.

She comes soft-eyed, with brooding breast,
   On swiftening wings of love ;
And England, to her bridal nest,
   Welcomes the gentle Dove.

She comes ; across the waters spread the sails ;
   She comes, to play her brave, uncommon part ;
The Princess who shall wear the name of Wales ;
   The Woman who shall win our England's heart.
The Nation's life up-leaps to meet her ;
And England with one voice goes forth to greet Her !

Our Lady cometh from the North,
   The tender and the true,
Whose fire of darkest glow hath rarest worth ;
For love more inly nestles in the North,
To give, like fire in frost, its fervours forth ;
   Whose flowers can keep their dew ;
And a look in its women's eyes is good
As the first fresh breath of the salt sea-flood,
   Or the bonniest blink of its blue :
And from its dark Fiords, with sails unfurled,
   Came those fair-haired Norsemen,
      The men that moved the world.

They were the pride and the darlings of Ocean,
  Rockt on her breast by a hundred storms ;
Tossed up with joyfullest motherly motion ;
  Caught to her heart again—claspt in her arms.
No Slaves of the Earth but Sea Kings, the rough
    rovers
  Took wings of the wind and flew over the foam.
Yet, the old True-hearts, like faithfullest lovers,
  Came back with the fruitfuller feeling of Home.

Come ! stir the Norse fire in us mightily !
Come, conquering hearts as they the heaving sea.
Come, wed the people with their Prince, and
    bless
Them from your neighbouring heaven of nobleness.
There's nothing like a Beauty of the Blood
To set the fashion of a loftier good !
There's nothing like a true and womanly Wife
To help a man, and make melodious life.
For, she can hold his heartstrings in her hand,
And play the tune her pleasure may command,
And cause his climbing soul to grow in stature,
Trying to reach the heights of her diviner nature.

Come in your beauty of promise ;
  Come in your maiden glee ;
Let your sunshine scatter from us
  The shadow of Misery.
Hearts in the dark have been aching,
But now the clouds are breaking.
Come as come the swallows
  Over the brightening sea,
And we know that summer follows
  With the sunny days to be.
Come and give us your glad good-morrow,
  The Joy-bells shall ring,
  And the merry birds sing ;
Dumbly drooping, the Bird of Sorrow
  Shall hide his old head under his wing.

And now a shining Vision blooms ;
  I see the rich procession glide
Serenely 'twixt the swaling plumes,
  All nodding in their pride :

Some gate of Dreamland opens wide ;
  We, for a moment, catch the sight

Within—the beauty of the Bride ;
   Her maidens all in white !

Walking with sweet precision, she
   Moves slowly onward, softly nigher
The Altar ; meek in purity,
   Yet filled with stately fire.

The dawn upon her sweet young face,
   The dewy spring-light in her eyes,
And round about her form of grace
   The airs of paradise.

But lo ! a shadow dims the scene !
   We lift our eyes and sadly see
How lonely stands the wistful Queen ;
   No leaning-place hath she,

Who, in her darkness seeks to hide,
   While the wed pair move whitely on
As swans go gliding side by side,
   And all their splendours sun.

O Widow's gloom ! O wedding joys !
   O white fringe to the Mourning-pall !
With the dead Father's hovering voice
   In music over all !

This world is but a newer paradise,
To that glad spirit looking thro' the eyes
Of Love, that sees all bright things dancing toward
It, gaily coming of their own accord.
For 'tis as tho' the lightsome heart should climb
Up in the head, to look from height sublime
And sing, and swing as it would never drop—
The merry reveller in the tall tree-top !
Where Life is with such lofty gladness crowned,
And all the Pleasures dance in starry circle round.
But may this love be true as Hers who sees
Ye, like a smiling future, at her knees :
The Wife who held God's gifts the richest wealth ;
Our Queen of Home who sweetened England's
        health ;
The Widow in whose face we lookt to see
That great black cloud of our calamity
On the side nearest heaven, and markt her rise
In stature, calm to meet her sacrifice :
As one with faith to feel Death's darkness brings
Almighty Love on overshadowing wings.

True love is no mere incense that will swim
Up from the heart a lover's eyes to dim,

But, such a light as gives the jewel-spark
To meanest things it looks on in their dark, —
A spring of heaven welling warm to bless
And sanctify each grain of earthiness.
True love will make true life, and glorify
Ye very proudly in the nation's eye.
Ah, Prince, a-many hopes up-fold the wing
Within the Marriage-nest to which ye bring
Your Bride, the life ye live there will be rolled
Through endless echoes, mirrored manifold.

We charge you, when you look on your young Wife,
And watch the ascending brightness of new life
In the sweet eyes that double the sweet soul,
That ye forget not others' dearth and dole.
   Just now, the north wind wails
      As though the cold were crying
    Over the hills and over the dales,
    And sinking hearts know well what ails
      The sound of the wintry sighing :
      It bears the moan of the dying ;
    Dying down in the starving Shires,
    Without food, and without fires.

The bitter nights are cruel cold,
    One cannot help but wake, and think
Of the poor milch-lambs of the human fold
    That have no milk to drink.

A Royal Worker to his grave went down
A little year ago, without his crown.
He dreamed the time would come when Rich and
    Poor
Might shake hands, strove to open wide the door.
He tried to till our waste-land,—sought to see
It glad in good, the stern world Poverty.
His was a heart that nobly beat to bless,
And heaved with double-breasted bounteousness
Like very woman's.
                    But, 'tis ever so ;
He's gone where all our golden sunsets go ;
Gone from us !   Yet his memory makes a light,
    Enriching life with tints of pictured bloom,
Like firelight warm upon the walls of night,
    An inner glow against the outer gloom.
Do thou but live, and work as Albert willed,
And he shall smile in heaven to see his dream
    fulfilled.

Heroic deeds of toil are to be done,
And lofty palms of peace are to be won.
Life may be followed by a fame that rings
With nobler music than the Battle sings,
When Death, astride the black Guns, laughs to see
That flashing out of souls, and grins triumphantly.

Love England, Prince ; for Christ's sake may ye be
Loyal to her, the glorious, great, and free !
Bear high the banner of her peerless fame,
And let the evil-doers fear her name.
We joy to serve her, least of all the race ;
Yours is the prize to fill her foremost place.

Like some proud River, stretching forth before ye
    Through all the land, your widening way doth lie,
Brimming and blessing as it rolls in glory,
    Broadening and brightening till it reach the sky.
A splendid Vision ! the green corn looks gay ;
    The Bird of Happiness sings overhead :
And may the autumn uplands far away
    Rise with their Harvest ripe in Evening's red ;
Your crescent Honey-Moon laugh out above
The gathered Sheaves it gilds, at full, with love.

PICTURES IN THE FIRE.

PICTURES IN THE FIRE.

OLD Winter blows, and whistles hard,
 To keep his fingers warm ; while I
Shut out the cold night, frosty-starred,
 Bleak earth and bitter sky ;
And to the Fireplace nestle nigher,
And gaze on pictures in the Fire.

It has a soft, blithe, murmuring glow,
 As if it crooned a cradle-song ;
Yet whispers of some awful woe
 Are on each flaming tongue
That may have licked up human life,
Quick, ruddy as a murderer's knife !

I see the Dead Men underground,
   Just as they found them rank on rank;
Old Mothers—Young Wives—red-eyed round
   The Corpses brought to bank;
I see the mournful phantoms flit
About the mouth of Hartley Pit;

And that poor Widow above the rest
   So eminent in Suffering's crown,
Who wearing sorrow's loftiest crest
   Is bowed the lowliest down;
Poor Widow with her Coffins seven,
Look down on Her, dear God in Heaven!

I hear that crash with sinking heart—
   Eternity has broken through!
I see him play His Hero part,
   That leader tried and true,
Who faithful stood to his last breath,
And fell betwixt them and their death.

I hear him bid them trim their lamps—
   For Light hath not gone out in Heaven!
And thro' the dark, above the damps,
   He beacons them to haven:

Long in his eyes had lived the light
That should make starry such a Night.

I see the strong man's agony,
   That seeks to rend his ghastly shroud ;
The touch of solemn radiancy
     That kindles through the cloud ;
The trust that earned a nobler doom
Than such a death in such a tomb ;

The valour that invisibly
   Lifted the bosom like a targe ;
The hidden forces that must be
     Ready for Life's last charge !
And all the bravery brave in vain,
And all the majesty of pain :

Visions of the old Home that flash
   With all the mind's last mortal power ;
The tears that burn their way, to wash
     A soul white in an hour,
When thoughts of God go deeper than
The Devil at His utmost can.

z

I hear the poor faint heart's low cry
   That sickens at the sight of Doom ;
The prayer of those who feel it nigh,
    And groping through the gloom !
They cower together hand-in-hand,
At the dark door of the dark land.

Ghostly and far-away life seems
   To one returning from a swound ;
And sharp the sorrow comes in dreams
    When we are helpless bound ;
But deathliest swoons, or ghastliest nights,
Have no such sounds, or spirit-sights.

The waiting human world is near,
   Yet farther off than Heaven for them
Who bow the doomëd head, to bear
    Death's cruel diadem,
With farewell words of solemn cheer
And love for those who cannot hear :

Old heads with hair like spray above
   A tossed and troubled sea of life ;
Young hearts, just kissed to the quick by Love.
    That leave a one-day wife !

O pathos of a hopeless fate !
O pain of those left desolate !

'Tis brave to die in Battle's flash,
    For the dear country we adore—
Struck breathless 'mid the glorious crash,
    When banners wave before
The fading eyes, and at the ears
We are caught by following Victory's cheers !

And sailor-blood that on the waves
    Can feel the Mother's heaving breast—
True sailor-blood no wailing craves
    Over *its* place of rest,
When souls first taste eternity
In those last kisses of the Sea :

And Death oft comes with kind release
    To win a smile from those that lie
Where they may feel the blessèd breeze,
    And look up at the sky,
And drink in, with their latest sigh,
A little air for strength to die :

But, 'tis a fearful thing to be
  Instantly buried alive; fast-bound
In cold arms of Eternity
    That clasp the breathing round,
And hold them, though their Comrades call
And dig with efforts useless all.

A tear for those who, in that night,
  Went down so unavailingly;
A cheer for those who fought our fight,
    And missed the victory !
Peace to the good true hearts that gave
A moral glory to that grave !

We know not how amid the gloom
  Some jewel of the just outshone;
With precious sparkle lit the tomb
    And led the hopeless on
To hope, and showed the only way
To find God's hand and reach his day.

We know not how in that quick hour
  Some poor uncultured human clod
May have put forth its one sweet flower,
    Acceptable to God ;

Or how the touch of Death revealed
Some buried beauty life concealed:

We know not how the Dove of peace
   Came brooding on the fluttering breast,
To make the fond life-yearnings cease,
     And fold them up for rest';
And into shining shape the soul
Burst, like the flame from out the coal:

We only know the watch-fires burned
   Long in their eyes for human aid,
And failed, and then to God they turned,
     And altogether prayed,
And that the deepest Mine may be,
For prayer, God's Whispering Gallery!

That Christ still hangs upon the Tree
   To smile beneath His thorns, and say
" *This night, Soul, thou shalt sup with me*,"
     In His old loving way;
And suffering men get back to God
By that same path the Saviour trod.

Deep, dark the deathly River is,
  Yet on before us walketh Christ !
His brightness over that abyss
  Is moving in the mist.
If they who pass the bridge of Dread
Look up, He goeth overhead !

Dear God, be very pitiful
  To these poor toiling slaves of men :
Be gracious if their hearts be dull
  With darkness of their den :
'Tis hard for flowers of Heaven to grow
Down where the earth-flowers cannot blow.

Their lives are as the Candle-snuff,
  Black in the midst of its own light !
Let hard hands plead for spirits rough—
  They work so much in night.
Be merciful, they breathe their breath
So close to danger, pain, and death.

The love-mist in a Father's eye
  Must rise, and soften much that's rude

In his poor children—magnify
 The least faint gleam of good !
O find some place for human worth
In Heaven, when it has failed on Earth.

GARIBALDI AT ASPROMONTE.

THE Lion is down, and how the Dogs will run !
  Something above the level is their delight
  For insult.   Asses lift the hoof to smite ;
The Birds of darkness hoot, "HIS DAY IS DONE."

" *Would he had kept his attitude sublime !*"
  Cry some.   " *With crossed arms held his heart at
      rest,*
  And left us his grand likeness at its best,
High on a hill up which the world might climb !"

" *Better for all had he been sooner shrined ;*
  The old true heart, and very foolish head.
  A model Man ; especially if dead :
Perfect as some Greek Statue—and, as blind."

GARIBALDI AT ASPROMONTE.

THE Lion is down, and how the Dogs will run!
    Something above the level is their delight
  For insult.   Asses lift the hoof to smite;
The Birds of darkness hoot, "HIS DAY IS DONE."

" *Would he had kept his attitude sublime!* "
    Cry some.   " *With crossed arms held his heart at*
        rest,
    And left us his grand likeness at its best,
High on a hill up which the world might climb! "

" *Better for all had he been sooner shrined;*
    The old true heart, and very foolish head.
    A model Man; especially if dead:
Perfect as some Greek Statue—and, as blind."

Friends talk of *failure:* and I know how he
   Will slowly lift his loving sincere eyes,
   And look them thro' with mournful, strange
      surprise,
Until they shrink and feel 'tis Italy

That fails instead.
          The words they came to speak
   Will shrink back awed by his majestic calm.
   His wounds are such as bleed immortal balm,
And he is strong again ; the friends are weak.

It is not failure to be thus struck down
   By Brothers who obeyed their Foe's command,
   And in the darkness lopped the saving hand
Put forth to reach their Country her last crown !

He only sought to see her safely home ;
   The tragic trials end, the sufferings cease,
   In wedded oneness and completing peace ;
Then bow his old grey head and die in Rome.

It is not failure to be thus struck back—
   Caught in a Country's arms, claspt to her heart;
   She tends his wounds awhile, and then will start
Afresh.   Some precious drops mark out her track.

No failure ! Tho' the rocks dash into foam
   This first strength of a nation's new life-stream,
   'Twill rise—a Bow of Promise—that shall gleam
In glory over all the waves to come.

Christ did not fail because He found a cross.
   The work went on altho' the Saviour died
   With two poor malefactors at His side.
Eternal gain repays such human loss !

We miss a footstep thinking " *Here's a stair*,"
   In some uncertain way we darkly tread;
   But God's enduring skies are overhead,
And Spirits step their surest oft in air.

His ways are not as our ways ; the new birth
   At cost of the old life is sometimes given :
   To-day God crowns the Martyrs in his heaven ;
To-morrow whips their murderers on our earth.

You take back Garibaldi to a prison?
   Why that may be the very road to Rome !
   They would have said " *She croucheth to her doom*,"
If Italy in some shape had not risen.

I say 'twas God's voice bade him offer up
   Himself for Aspromonte's sacrifice ;
   So, to that height, his countrymen might rise :
For them he freely drank the bitter cup.

It is a faith too many still receive—
   Since that false prophecy of old went forth—
   " *The tribe of Judas yet shall rule the earth;* "
But he is one that never would believe.

His vision is most clear where ours is dim.
   The mystic spirit of eternity
   That slumbers in us deep and dreamingly,
Was ever quick and more awake in him.

And, like a lamp across some pathless heath,
   A light shone thro' his eyes no night could quench ;
   The winds might make it flicker, rains might
      drench,
Nothing could dim it save the dark of death.

And if his work's unfinished in the flesh,
   Why, then his soul will join the noble Dead,
   And toil till all shall be accomplishëd,
And Italy hath burst this Devil's mesh.

Easier to conquer kingdoms than to breed
   A man like Garibaldi, whose great name
   Hath fenced his Country with his glorious fame,
Worth many armies in her battle-need.

His is the royal heart that never quails,
   But always conquers; wounded, lying low,
   He never was so dear as he is now:
They bind him, and more strongly he prevails.

Greater to-day than Emperor or King,
   Altho' for throne they seat him in the dust;
   The express image of sublimest Trust,
Crown'd, consecrated by his suffering,

With sovereignty that overtops success!
   Nothing but Heaven might reach his patriot brow,
   And lo, the Crown of Thorns is on it now,
With higher guerdon than our world's caress.

The vision of all his glory fills our eyes,
   And with one heart expectant nations throb
   Around him ; with one mighty prayer they sob,
And wait God's answer to this sacrifice,—

Praying for one more chance at turn of tide ;
   One blow for Rome ere many setting suns ;
   One stroke for Venice kneeling 'neath her guns ;
All Italy abreast, and at his side :

That he may stand as Wellington once stood
   Victor upon the hard-won Pyrenees,
   With France below him, offering on her knees
The White Flower Peace, sprung from her Root of
     Blood.

PRIDEAUX AT MAGDALA.

NO Cross of Valour hath the Muse to give
    His faithful breast, but she may bid him live
  In hearts of grateful glow,
Who went to bear his Message with last breath,
Nor changëd countenance at sight of Death,
  When Napier bade him go.

England, our Helen, watching from the wall
To cheer us fighting, mourn us if we fall,
  O'erlooks her gallant Son !
She hath so many lofty memories
To keep her lifted gaze; a deed like this
  So many would do—have done :

He did it ! that poor Private in the " Buffs," *
Though only one of her neglected " roughs,"—
   All English, life and limb :
He would not bow his head except to die ;
He could not let our England's image lie
   Dishonoured, shamed in him !

Duty, not Glory, is our proud pass-word,
Who ask that we may prove for England's sword
   True steel at need—no more.
Yet worthy of his guerdon is Prideaux,
As if on board they had borne him, lying low
   For us who were safe on shore.

That large content with death for England's sake
In narrower hearts a nobler life shall wake
   To breathe with ampler breath,
And some poor soul, caught in as bitter strait,
Shall think of him, and sternly face its fate—
   Go on, and out-face Death !

---

  * Moyse, an English soldier killed in China because he would not
perform the *kotou*, said he would not prostrate himself before any
Chinaman alive—would see them, &c. &c.

Blow, winds of God ! and stir us to the root,
Shake down all wormy and unworthy fruit,
   There's new life in your breeze !
Traitors may talk of England going down
(In quicksands that their coward selves have
     sown)—
   She swims in hearts like these !

SONGS AND OTHER BREVITIES.

SYLVIA MAY.

" HEART *of mine, so longing for rest,*
    Better to build thy love-lined Nest
On a storm-swung bough than a Woman's breast."

But this heart of mine still sayeth me, " Nay ; "
Shows me the picture of Sylvia May :
Wilful heart must have its way !

" *Heart of mine, far wiser 'twould be*
To build thy nest on a wave of the sea,
Tossed and troubled perpetually."

But this heart of mine still sayeth me, " Nay ; "
And whispers the name of Sylvia May :
Foolish heart will have its way !

" Never was love I think like mine;
Never was woman so nearly divine;
Never could lives more perfectly twine."

And this heart of mine it murmureth, " Yea ; "
Wilful heart must have its way—
When will you marry me, Sylvia May?

PARTING.

TOO fair, I may not call thee mine :
 Too dear, I may not see
Those eyes with bridal-beacons shine ;
 Yet, Darling, keep for me—
Empty and husht, and safe apart,
One little corner of thy heart !

Thou wilt be happy, dear ! and bless
 Thee ; happy mayst thou be.
I would not make thy pleasure less ;
 Yet, Darling, keep for me,
My life to light, my lot to leaven,
One little corner of thy Heaven !

Good-bye, dear heart! I go to dwell
　A weary way from thee:
Our first kiss is our last farewell;
　Yet, Darling, keep for me—
Who wander outside in the night,
One little corner of thy light!

OLD FRIENDS.

WE just shake hands at meeting
    With many that come nigh ;
We nod the head in greeting
    To many that go by,—
But welcome through the gateway
    Our few old friends and true ;
Then hearts leap up, and straightway
    There's open house for you,
              Old Friends,
    Wide open house for you !

The surface will be sparkling,
    Let but a sunbeam shine ;
Yet in the deep lies darkling
    The true life of the wine !

The froth is for the many,
  The wine is for the few ;
Unseen, untoucht of any,
  We keep the best for you,
                Old Friends,
  The very best for you.

The Many cannot know us ;
  They only pace the strand,
Where at our worst we show us—
  The waters thick with sand !
But out beyond the leaping
  Dim surge 'tis clear and blue ;
And there, Old Friends, we are keeping
  A waiting calm for you,
                Old Friends,
  A sacred calm for you.

AUTUMN SONG.

THE summer days are ended;
  The after-glow is gone;
The nights grow long and eerie;
  The winds begin to moan;
The pleasant leaves are fading;
  The bonny swallows flee;
Yet welcome is the Winter
  That brings my Love to me.

No voice of bird now ripples
  The air; no wood-walk rings!
But in my happy bosom
  The soul of Music sings.

It sings of clearest heaven,
   And summers yet to be ;
Then welcome is the Winter
   That brings my Love to me.

A world of gathered sunshine
   Is this warm heart of mine,
Where life hath heapt the fruitage,
   And love hath hid the wine.
And though there's not a flower
   In field, nor leaf on tree ;
Yet welcome is the Winter
   That brings my Love to me.

LOFTY AND LOWLY.

I LOVE a lady all so far above
    Me, she can never hear the name of love ;
I only whisper to my heart in low
Dark sayings what my lady must not know ;
But, had I only a minute's space to live,
And she beside me, I would pray her give
Me on the mouth one dear and holy kiss ;
And straightway a warm stream of paradise
Would gush and gladden all the gulf of death,
A calm of blessëd faces take mine eyes ;
A hurricane of harpings take my breath :
All heavën would bend brooding down to meet
Me, in that gracious stooping of my Sweet ;
And, at her touch, my soul should enter bliss.

HEIGH-HO !

HEIGH-HO ! She will never be mine :
    Never ! never. I know
The grasp of gold
My Jewel will hold :
    She is Lofty and I am Low.

Heigh-ho ! but my heart like a Bird
    On wings of the night will go,
To make its love-nest
In that heaven of her breast,
    'Neath the heaven of her eyes all aglow.

Heigh-ho ! in dreams she is mine,
    All mine : and how can I know
But she loves *me* in dream,
With no drawn sword a-gleam,
    'Twixt the kissing of Lofty and Low ?

LOVE'S WESTWARD HO!

PLEASANT it is, sweet Wife of mine,
    As by my side thou art,
To sit and see thy dear eyes shine
    With bonfires of the heart !
And young Love smiles so sweet and sly,
    From warm and balmy deeps,
As under-leaf the fruit may try
    To hide, yet archly peeps :
Gliding along in our fairy boat,
    With prospering skies above,
Over the sea of time we float
    To another New World of Love.

B B

One of God's Darlings is our Guide ;
    Ah, how it makes us lean,
Hearts beating lovingly side by side
    That nothing may come between.
And as yon ring of Stars doth fold
    Our world, so is it given
To this wee ring of wedding gold
    To clasp us round with heaven :
Gliding along in our fairy boat,
    With prospering skies above,
Over the sea of time we float
    To another New World of Love.

HOME SONG.

THE Larch is snooding her tresses
    In a twine of the daintiest green ;
With fresh spring-breath the Hawthorn heaves
    His breast to the sunny sheen.
A shower of spring-green sprinkles the Lime ;
    A shower of spring-gold the Broom ;
And each rathe tint of the tender time
    Wakes the wish that my Lady were Home.

In the Coppice, the dear Primroses
    Are the smile of each dim green nook,
Gravely gladsome ; sunny but cool
    With the sound of the gurgling brook.

And by the wayside, in a burst of delight,
  From the world of fairy and gnome,
All the flowers are crowding to see the sight
  At their windows.   My Lady come Home !

The Country's growing glorious
  Quietly day by day ;
The colour of April comes and goes
  In a blush to meet the May.
And the spring-rains steal from their heaven of
    shade,
  In a veil of tender gloam,
With a splendid sparkle for every blade.
  Dear my Lady come Home !

The Spirit of Gladness floating
  Goes up in a sound of song :
Robin sings in the rich eve-lights ;
  The Throstle all day long :
The Lark in his heaven that soars above
  Each morn with a distant dome ;
All sweet ! but sweeter the voice we love.
  Come Home, my Lady, come Home !

Your Apple-blooms are fragrant
   Beyond the breath of the South ;
Every bud, for an airy kiss,
   Is lifting a rosy wee mouth.
A greener glory hour by hour,
   And a peep of ruddier bloom,
But the leafy world waiteth its human flower.
   Dear my Lady come Home !

Our thoughts are as the Violets
   Around the Ash-tree root,
That breathe the earliest hints of Spring
   At their lofty lady's foot,
And wonder why she still delays—
   When the sea of life is a-foam
With flowers—to crown her in these glad days.
   Come Home, my Lady, come Home !

Come ! feel the deepening dearness
   About the grand old place.
Come ! let us see the cordial smile
   Once more in our Lady's face.

Winter was dreary : of waiting we weary :
   Best of all joy-bringers, come !
Spread bonny white sails ! blow balmy spring-gales !
   And bring my Lady Home !

THE WHITE CHILD.

MOTHERS of Children three ;
    Two of them ruddy with glee ;
One your White Child, your pearl !
Do you feel as I feel with my Girl ?
For I peer in her tender face,
And I fear that its light of grace
Is too still and too starry a birth
For our noisy, dim dwellings of Earth.
She looks like a natural Child
Of the heavens—too lustrous, too mild
For us.   Other Roses are blowing
While mine seems up-folding and going,—
Dreamily happy in going.

Yet on it more soft is the thorn
Than the tiniest little snail's-horn,
And golden at heart is the Morn
Of a day that may never be born.

Just a spirit of light is my Girl,
Seen thro' a body of pearl ;
A spirit of life that will fleet
Away, more on wings than on feet.
Her cheek is so waxenly thin,
As if deathward 'twere whitening in,
And the cloud of her flesh, still more white,
Were clearing till soul is in sight.
She leans as the wind-flowers stoop ;
All their loveliness seen as they droop !
Her eyes have the sweet native hue
Of the heaven they are melting into,
Blue as the Violets above
The grave of some tender babe-love
That back to us wistfully bring
The buried blue eyes with the Spring.
Her large eyes too liquidly glister !
Her mouth is too red.

Have they kissed her—
The Angels that bend down to pull
Our buds of the Beautiful,
And whispered their own little Sister?

O Mothers of Children three!
Two of them bright of blee;
One, your White Child, your pearl!
Do you feel as I feel with my Girl?
For I think I could give half her wealth
Of heaven for a little more health:
The halo of Saints for the simple
Blithe graces that dip in a dimple!
Nay, I feel in my heart I could revel
To see but a wee dash of devil;
A touch of the old Adam in her;
A glimpse of his fair fellow-sinner;
Any likeness of earth that would give
Me a promise my Darling should live.
O my love! O my life! O my Maker,
Take ME too, if Thou MUST take her!

CHILDREN AT PLAY.

" OPEN *your mouth and shut your eyes* "—
   Three little Maidens were saying—
"*And see what God sends you!*" little they thought
   He listened while they were playing !
So little we guess that a light light word
   At times may be more than praying.

" I," said Kate with the merry blue eyes,
   " *Would have lots of frolic and folly ;*"
" I," said Ciss with the bonny brown hair,
   " *Would have life always smiling and jolly ;* "
" *And I would have just what our Father may send,*"
   Said loveable little pale Polly.

Life came for the Two, with sweetnesses new
  Each morning in gloss and in glister.
But Our Father above, in a gush of great love,
  Caught up little Polly and kissed her.
And the Churchyard nestled another wee grave ;
  The Angels another wee Sister.

SLEEP-WALKING.

OFT in the night I am with you, Dear !
   I lean and listen your breathing to hear ;
Little you dream of any one near.

No one knoweth that I am gone ;
Curtains closely about me drawn,
When dreams dissolve at touch of Dawn.

Nobody meets me under the sky,
Only the staring Owl goes by
Softly as tho' the Night should sigh.

Under the moonlight, over the moss !
I need no bridge the river to cross,
Tho' winds awake and waters toss.

O sweet, so sweet the Nightingale's strain !
Is it her pleasure that works us pain,
Or her pain that with pleasure pierces the brain ?

Window or door I pass not thro':
The way I never could show to you
By day.   I enter as spirits do !

There you are ! lying cheek-on-palm,
Drinking of slumber's dewiest calm,
Filling your life with the rosiest balm.

The little wee bird that beats in the breast,
Hath folded its wings in a wee white nest,
Breathing the odours of sweet rest.

But the other night—see my blushes bloom—
Somehow I missed my way in the gloom,
And, thinking myself quite safe in your room,

I nestled my face, as I thought, in your bed
To kiss you, and—let me hide my head—
I kissed—I kissed—your Teacher instead.

AN APOLOGUE.

IN the olden day when Immortals
  Came oftener visibly down,
There went a Youth with an Angel
  Thro' the gate of an Eastern Town :
They passed a Dog by the road-side,
  Where dead and rotting it lay,
And the Youth, at the ghastly odour,
  Sickened and turned away.
He gathered his robes about him
  And hastily hurried thence :
But nought annoyed the Angel's
  Clear, pure, immortal sense.

By came a lady, lip-luscious,
   On delicate tinkling feet :
All the place grew glad with her presence,
   The air about her sweet ;
For she came in fragrance floating,
   And her voice most silverly rang ;
The Youth, to embrace her beauty,
   With all his being sprang.
A sweet, delightsome Lady :
   And yet the Legend saith,
The Angel, while he passed her,
   Shuddered and held *his* breath.

THE GLOW-WORM.

THE Apes found a Glow-worm,
  Shining in the night,—
A little drop of radiance
  Tenderly alight ;

Ho ! Ho ! shivered the Apes,
  Grinning all together,
We'll make a fire to warm us ;
  'Tis jolly cold weather.

With dry sticks and dead leaves,
  All the Apes came ;
Piled a heap and squatted round
  To blow it into flame !

But fire would not kindle so—
    Vain their wasted breath !
Only they blew out the glow—
    Put the worm to death.

Glow-worms were meant to shine ;
    Apes can't blow them hot,
Just to warm their foolish hands,
    Or boil their flesh-pot.

So the World would serve the Poet,
    With his light of love.
Probably his use may be
    Better known above.

MY NEIGHBOUR.

"LOVE *thou thy Neighbour*," we are told,
　　" *Even as Thyself.*" That creed I hold;
But love her more, a thousand-fold!

My lovely Neighbour; oft we meet
In lonely lane, or crowded street;
I know the music of her feet.

She little thinks how, on a day,
She must have missed her usual way,
And walked into my heart for aye:

Or how the rustle of her dress
Thrills thro' me like a soft caress,
With trembles of deliciousness.

Wee woman, with her smiling mien,
And soul celestially serene,
She passes me, unconscious Queen!

Her face most innocently good,
Where shyly peeps the sweet red blood:
Her form a nest of Womanhood!

Like Raleigh—for her dainty tread,
When ways are miry—I could spread
My cloak, but, there's my heart instead.

Ah, Neighbour, you will never know
Why 'tis my step is quickened so;
Nor what the prayer I murmur low.

I see you 'mid your flowers at morn,
Fresh as the rosebud newly born;
I marvel, can *you* have a thorn?

If so, 'twere sweet to lean one's breast
Against it, and, the more it prest,
Sing like the Bird that sorrow hath blest.

I hear you sing !   And thro' me Spring
Doth musically ripple and ring ;
Little you think I'm listening !

You know not, dear, how dear you be ;
All dearer for the secrecy :
Nothing, and yet a world to me.

So near, too ! you could hear me sigh,
Or see my case with half an eye ;
But must not.   There are reasons why.

The four following extracts are reproduced and retouched from the Author's last volume of poems, "Havelock's March," &c., published nine years ago; or, rather, secretly committed to the public—which secret, as Coleridge said of one of his publications, the public very faithfully kept. The Author learned too late that a prefatory Note had misled readers into looking on the book as a mere reprint of old matter, and so it passed nearly unnoticed by reviewers, and remains almost as " good as manuscript."

A LETTER IN BLACK.

A FLOATING on the fragrant flood
   Of Summer—fuller hour by hour ;
All the Spring-sweetness of the bud
   Crowned by the glory of the flower,—
My spirits with the season flowed.
   The air was all a breathing balm ;
The lake in flame of sapphire glowed ;
   The mountains lay in cloudless calm :

Green leaves were lusty ; roses blusht
   For pleasure in the golden time ;
The birds thro' all their feathers flusht
   For gladness of their marriage-prime :

Listless among the lilies I threw
  Me down, for coolness 'mid the sheen :
Heaven, one large smile of brooding blue ;
  Earth, one large smile of basking green.

A rich suspended shower of gold
  Laburnum o'er me hung its crown :
You look up heavenward and behold
  It glowing, coming in glory down !
There, as my thoughts of greenness grew
  To fruitage of a leafy dream—
There, friend, your letter thrilled me thro',
  And from the summer died the gleam.

The world, so pleasant to the sight,
  So full of voices blithe and brave,
And all her lamps of beauty alight
  With life ! I had forgot the Grave ;
And there it opened at my feet,
  Revealing a familiar face
Upturned, my whitened look to meet,
  And very patient in its place.

My poor bereaven friend! I know
    Not how to word it, but would bring
A little solace for your woe,
    A little love for comforting.
And yet the best that I can say
    Will only help to sum your loss.
I can but look above and pray—
    " God help my friend to bear his Cross."

I have felt something of your smart,
    And lost the dearest thing e'er wound
In love about a human heart:
    I too have life-roots under ground.
From out my soul hath leapt a cry
    For help! Nor God Himself could save.
And tears yet run that nought will dry
    Save Death's hand with the dust o' the grave.

God knows, and we may one day know,
    These hidden secrets of His love!
But now the stillness stuns us so;
    Darkly as in a dream we move:

The glad life-pulses come and go
    Over our head and at our feet :
Soft airs are sighing something low ;
    The flowers are saying something sweet.

And 'tis a merry world.   The Lark
    Is singing over the green corn.
Only the house and heart are dark ;
    Only the human world forlorn.
There, in the bridal-chamber lies
    A dear bed-fellow all in white :
That purple shadow under the eyes
    Where star-fire swam in liquid night.

Sweet, slippery silver of her talk ;
    The music of her laugh so dear,
Heard in home-ways and wedded walk
    For many and many a golden year :
The singing soul and shining face,
    Daisy-like glad by roughest road ;
Gone ! with a thousand dearnesses
    That hid themselves for us and glowed.

The waiting Angel, patient Wife,
    All thro' the battle at our side ;
That smiled her sweetness on our strife
    For gain, and it was sanctified.
When waves of trouble beat breast-high,
    And the heart sank, she poured a balm
That stilled them : and the saddest sky
    Made clear and starry with her calm.

And when the world with harvest ripe
    In all its golden fulness lay ;
And God, it seem'd, saw fit to wipe,
    Even on earth, all tears away :
The good true heart that bravely won,
    Must smile up in our face and fall ;
And all our happy days are done.
    And this the end ! And is this all ?

The bloom of bliss, the secret glow,
    That clothed without and inly curled,
All gone. We are left shivering now,
    Naked to the wide open world :

A shrivelled, withered world it is,
  So sad, and miserably cold;
Where be its vaunted braveries?
  Grown gray and miserably old!

Our joy was all a drunken dream.
  This is the truth at waking! We
Are swept out rootless by the stream
  And current of calamity—
Out on some lone and shoreless sea
  Of solitude so vast and deep,
As 'twere the wrong Eternity
  Where God is not, or gone to sleep.

It seems as tho' our Darling dead,
  Startled at Death's so sudden call,
With falling hands and dear bowed head
  Had, like a flower-filled lap, let fall
A hoard of treasures we have found
  Too late! So slow doth wisdom come!
We for the first time look around
  Remembering this is not our Home.

My friend, I see you with your cup
  Of tears and trembling—see you sit;
And long to help you drink it up,
  With useless longings infinite—
Sit rocking the old mournful thought,
  That on the heart's-blood will be nurst,
Unless the blessèd tears be brought;
  Unless the cloudy sorrows burst!

The little ones are gone to rest,
  And for a-while they will not miss
The Mother-wings above the nest;
  But thro' their slumber slides her kiss,
And, dreaming she has come, they start
  And toss wild arms for her caress,
With moanings that must thrill a heart
  In heaven with divine distress.

And Sorrow on your threshold stands,
  The Dark Ladye in gloomy pall:
I see her take you by the hands;
  I feel her shadow over all.

Hers is no warm and tender clasp !
   With silence solemn as the Night's,
And veilëd face, and spirit-grasp,
   She leads her Chosen up the heights :

The cloudy crags are cold and gray :
   You cannot scale them without scars :
So many Martyrs by the way
   Who never reacht her tower of stars !
But there her beauty shall be seen ;
   Her glittering face so proudly pure ;
And all her majesty of mien ;
   And all her guerdon shall be sure.

Well.   'Tis not written, God will give
   To His Belovëd only rest.
The hard life of the Cross they live,
   They strive, and suffer, and are blest.
The feet must bleed to reach their throne ;
   The brow must burn before it bear
One of the crowns that may be won
   By workers, for immortal wear.

Dear friend, life beats tho' buried 'neath
   Its long black vault of night! And see,
There trembles thro' this dark of death,
   Starlight of immortality!
And yet shall dawn the eternal day
   To kiss the eyes of them that sleep;
And He shall wipe all tears away
   From tired eyes of them that weep.

'Tis something for the poor bereaven,
   In such a weary world of care,
To think that we have friends in heaven;
   Who helpt us here, may aid us there!
These yearnings for them set our Arc
   Of Being widening more and more,
In circling sweep thro' outer dark
   To day more perfect than before.

So much was left unsaid.   The soul
   Must live in other worlds to be;
On earth we cannot grasp the whole,
   For that Love has eternity.

Love deep as death and rich as rest ;
   Love that was love with all Love's might ;
Level to needs the lowliest ;
   Cannot be less Love at full-height !

Tho' earthly forms be far apart,
   Spirit to spirit nestles nigher ;
The music chords the same at heart
   Tho' one voice range an octave higher.
Eyes watch us that we cannot see ;
   Lips warn us which we may not kiss ;
They wait for us, and starrily
   Lean towards us from Heaven's lattices.

We cannot see them face to face,
   But love is nearness.   And they love
Us yet, nor change, with change of place,
   In their more steadfast world above,
Where love, once leal, hath never ceased,
   And dear eyes never lose their shine,
And there shall be a Marriage Feast,
   Where Christ shall once more make the wine.

OUR. MAID MARIAN.

SPRING comes with violet eyes unveiled,
   Her fragrant lips apart;
And Earth smiles up as tho' she held
   Most honeyed thoughts at heart.
But nevermore will Spring arise
Dancing in sparkles of *her* eyes.

A gracious wind low-breathing comes
   From out the fields of God;
The old lost Eden newly blooms
   From out the sunny sod.
My buried joy stirs with the earth,
And tries to sun *its* sweetness forth.

D D

The trees move in their slumbering,
   Dreaming of one that's near ;
Put out their feelers for the Spring,
   To wake, and find her here !
My spirit on the threshold stands,
And stretches out its waiting hands,

Then goeth from me in a stream
   Of yearning ; wave on wave
Slides thro' the stillness of a dream,
   To little Marian's grave :
For all the miracle of Spring
My long-lost child will never bring.

Where blooms the golden crocus-burst,
   And Winter's tenderling,
There lies our little Snowdrop ! first
   Of Flowers in our love's spring !
How all the year's young beauties blow
About her there, I know, I know.

The Blackbird with his warble wet,
   The Thrush with reedy thrill,
Open their hearts to Spring, and let
   The influence have its will !

Tho' all around the Spring hath smiled,
She seems to have kissed where lies our child.

In purple shadow and golden shine
   Old Arthur's Seat is crown'd;
Like shapes of Silence crystalline
   The great white clouds sail round!
The Dead at rest the long day thro'
Lie calm against the pictured blue.

O Marian, our Maid Marian,
   So strange it seems to me!
That you, the household's darling one,
   So soon should cease to be.
Ah, was it that our praying breath
Might kindle heavenward fires of faith?

So much forgiven for your sake
   When bitter words were said,
And little arms about the neck
   With blessings bowed the head!
So happy as we might have been,
Our hearts more close with you between.

Dear early Dew-drop ! such a gleam
    Of sun from heaven you drew,
We little thought that smiling beam
    Would drink our precious dew !
But back to heaven our dew was kissed,
We saw it pass in mournful mist.

We bore her beauty in our breast,
    As heaven bears the Dawn.
We brooded over her dear nest,
    Still close and closer drawn ;
Hearts thrilled and listened, watched and throbbed
And strayed not,—yet the nest was robbed !

" *Stay yet a little while, Beloved !* "
    In vain our prayerful breath :
Across heaven's lighted window moved
    The shadow of black Death.
In vain our hands were stretcht to save ;
There closed the gateways of the Grave !

Could my death-vision have darkened up
    In her sweet face, my child :
I scarce should see the bitter cup,
    I could have drank and smiled :

Blessing her with my last-wrung breath,
Dear Angel in my dream of death !

Her memory is like music we
　　Have heard some singer sing,
That thrills life thro', and echoingly
　　Our hearts for ever ring ;
We try it o'er and o'er again,
But ne'er recall the wondrous strain.

My full heart like a river runs,
　　Lying awake o' nights ;
I see her with the Shining Ones
　　Upon the shining heights.
And a wee Angel-face will peep
Down starlike thro' the veil of sleep.

My yearnings try to get them wings
　　And float me up afar,
As in the dawn the sky-lark springs
　　To reach some distant Star
That all night long swam down to him
In brightness, but at morn grew dim.

She is a spirit of light that leavens
　　The darkness where we wait ;
And starlike opens in the heavens
　　A little golden gate !
O may we wake and find her near
When work and sleep are over here !

No sweetness to this world of ours
　　Is without purpose given,
The fragrance that goes up from Flowers
　　May be their soul in heaven.
We saw Heaven in her face, may we
Her future face in Heaven see.

In some far spring of brighter bloom,
　　More life and ampler breath,
My bud hath burst the folding gloom,
　　A-flower from dusty death !
We wonder will she be much grown ?
And how will her new name be known ?

I saw her ribboned robe this morn,
　　Mine own lost little child ;
Wee shoes her tiny feet had worn,
　　And then my heart grew wild.

We only trust ourselves to peep
In on them when we want to weep.

But hearts will break or eyes must weep,
   And so we bend above
These treasures of old days that keep
   The fragrance of young love.
Our harvest-field tho' reapt and bare
Hath yet a patient gleaner there.

I never think of her sweet eyes
   In dusky death now dim,
But waters of my heart will rise,
   And there they smile and swim,
Forget-me-nots so blue, so dear,
Swim in the waters of a tear.

How often in the days gone by
   She lifted her dear head,
And stretcht wee arms for me to lie
   Down in her little bed.
And cradled in my happy breast
Was carried softly into rest.

And now when life is sore oppressed
  And runs with weary wave,
I long to lay me down and rest
  In little Marian's grave ;
To smile as peaceful as she smiled—
For I am now the nestling child.

Immortal Love, a spirit of bliss
  And brightness, moves above,
While here forever Sorrow is
  The shadow cast by Love,
But love for her no sorrow will bring
And no more tearful leaves-taking.

No passing troubles on their march
  Will leave sad foot-prints now ;
No trials strain the tender arch
  Of that white baby brow.
No cares to cloud, no tears to come,
That rob the cheek of pearly bloom.

All sweetest shapes that Beauty wears
  Are round about her drawn ;
Auroral bloom, and vernal airs,
  And blessings of the dawn ;

All loveliness that ne'er grows less ;
Time cannot touch her tenderness.

One sparkle of immortal light
    Our love for her shall shine
In the dew-drop that nestles white
    At heart with gleam divine,
But vanishes from Death's cold clasp
When he the flower of life doth grasp.

The patient calm that comes with years,
    Hath made us cease to fret ;
Only at times in sudden tears
    Dumb hearts will quiver yet :
And each one turns the face and tries
To hide WHO looks thro' parent eyes.

THE RELIEF.

(FROM " HAVELOCK'S MARCH.")

THERE Lucknow lies before them — all its
 pageantry unrolled.
Against the smiling sapphire gleam her tops of
 lighted gold.
Each royal wall is fretted all with frostwork and
 with fire ;
A glory of colour, jewel-rich, that makes a splen-
 dour-pyre,
As wave on wave the wonder breaks ; the pointed
 flames burn higher
On dome of Mosque and Minaret, on pinnacle and
 spire :

Fairy creations, seen mid-air, that in their pleasaunce
wait,

Like wingèd creatures sitting just outside their
heaven-gate.

The city in its beauty lies, with flowers about her feet :

Green fields and goodly gardens make the foul thing
fair and sweet !

The Bugle rings out for the march, and with its
proudest thrill,

Goes to the heart of Havelock's men, working its
lordly will ;

Making their spirits thrill as leaves are thrill'd in
some wild wind ;

Hunger and heartache, weariness and wounds, all
left behind.

Their sufferings all forgotten now, as in the ranks
they form,

And every soul in stature rose to wrestle with the
storm !

All silent. What was hid at heart could not be
said in words.

With faces set for Lucknow, ground to sharpness,
keen as swords.

A tightening twitch all over ! a grim glistening in
    the eye ;

" Forward !" and on their way they strode, to dare,
    and do, and die.

Hope whispers at the ear of some that they shall
    meet again

And clasp their long-lost darlings, after all the toil
    and pain.

A-many know that they will sleep to-night among
    the slain

And many a cheek will bloom no more for all the
    tearful rain.

And some have only vengeance, but to-day 'tis
    bitter-sweet !

And there goes Havelock, his the aim too lofty for
    defeat.

With steady tramp the Column treads, true as the
    firm heart's beat,

Strung for its headlong murderous march thro' that
    long fatal street.

All ready to win a soldier's grave, or do the daring
    deed,

But not a man that fears to die for England in her
    need.

The masked Artillery raked the road and ploughed
them front and flank.

Some gallant fellow every stride was stricken from
the rank.

But, as he staggered, in his place another sternly
stepped,

And firing fast as they could load their onward
way they kept.

Now, give them the good bayonet ! with England's
fiercest foes,

Strong arm, cold steel will do it, in the wildest,
bloodiest close !

And now the bayonets abreast go sternly up the
ridge,

And with another charge they take the guns and
clear the bridge.

One good home-thrust ! and surely as the dead in
doom are sure

They send them where the British cheer can trouble
them no more.

The fire is biting bitterly ; onward the battle rolls.

Grim Death is glaring at them, from ten thousand
hiding-holes.

Death stretches up from earth to heaven, spreading
    his darkness round ;
Death piles the heaps of helplessness face-downward
    to the ground :
Death flames from sudden ambuscades where all
    was still and dark ;
Death swiftly speeds on whizzing wings the bullets
    to their mark ;
Death from the doors and windows, all around and
    overhead,
Darts with his cloven, fiery tongues, incessant,
    quick and red.
Death everywhere : Death in all sounds, and, thro'
    its smoke of breath,
Victory beckons at the end of long, dark lanes of
    death.

Another charge, another cheer, another battery
    won.
And in a whirlwind of fierce fire the fight goes roar-
    ing on !
Into the very heart of hell, with comrades falling
    fast,
Thro' all that tempest terrible, the glorious remnant
    passed.

No time to help a dear old friend, but where the
wounded fell,

They knew it was all over and they lookt a last
farewell.

And dying eyes slow-setting in a cold and stony
stare,

Turned upward, see a map of murder scribbled on
the air

With crossing flames, and others read their fiery,
fearful fate,

In dark, swart faces waiting for them, whitening
with their hate.

O proudly men will march to death, when Havelock leads them on ;

Thro' all the storm he sat his horse as he were cut
in stone.

But now his look grows dark, his eye gleams with
uneasy flash ;

" *On, for the Residency, we must make a last brave
dash ;*"

And on dasht Highlander and Sikh, thro' a sea of
fire and steel ;

On with the lion of their strength, our first in glory,
Neill.

It seemed the face of heaven grew black, so close it
    held its breath

Thro' all the glorious agony of that long march of
    death.

The round shot tears, the bullets rain ; dear God,
    outspread thy shield ;

Put forth thy red right arm for them ; Thy sword of
    sharpness wield !

One wave breaks forward on the shore, and one falls
    helpless back.

Again they club their wasted strength and fight like
    " *Hell-fire Jack.*"*

And, ever as fainter grows the fire of that intrepid
    band,

Again they grasp the bayonet as 'twere Salvation's
    hand.

They leap the broad deep trenches ; rush thro'
    archways streaming fire ;

Every step some brave heart bursts, heaving deliver-
    ance nigher.

---

* Sobriquet of Captain Olpherts.

" *I'm hit*," cries one—" *You'll take me on your back,
    old comrade; I*
*Should like to see their dear white faces once before I
    die!*
My body may save you from the shot."
                  His comrade bore him on ;
But, ere they reacht the Bailie Guard, the hurrying
    soul was gone.

And now the Gateway arched in sight ; the last
    grim tussle came ;
One moment makes immortal ! dead or living, end-
    less fame !
They heard the voice of fiery Neill that for the last
    time thrilled :
" *Push on, my men, 'tis getting dark:*" he sat where
    he was killed.
Another frantic surge of life, and plunging o'er the bar
Right into harbour hurling goes their whirling wave
    of war,
And breaks in mighty thunders of reverberating
    cheers,
Then dances on in frolic foam of kisses, blessings,
    tears.

E E

Stabbed by mistake, one native cries, with the last
  breath he draws :
" *Welcome, my friends ; never you mind, it's all for*
  the good cause."

How they had leaned and listened as the battle
  sounded nigher ;
How they had strained their eyes to see them
  coming crown'd with fire ;
Till in the flashing street below they heard them
  pant for breath,
And then the English faces smiled clear from the
  cloud of death,
And iron grasp met tender clasp : wan weeping
  women fold
Their dear Deliverers, down whose long brown
  beards the big tears rolled.
Another such a meeting will not be on this side
  heaven !
The little wine they have hoarded to the last drop
  shall be given
To those, who, in their mortal need, fought on thro'
  fearful odds ;
Bled for them ; reacht them ; saved them ; less like
  men than glorious gods.

ENGLAND.

(FROM " ENGLAND IN 1859.")

YOU lovers of our England, do but look
   On this dear Country over whose fair face
God droopt a bridal-veil of tender mist,
That she might keep her beauty virginal,
And he might see her thro' a softer glory:
So very meek and reverent doth she stand
Within this shadow soft of Love Divine,
A sacred sweetness in her good, gray eyes;
A tenderer radiance kindling in her clouds;
A dewier lustre in her grass and flowers;
More loveable, and not as brighter lands
Whose bolder beauty stares up in Heaven's face.

Look on her now, this Darling of the Sea,
Smiling upon her image in its calm,

As Beauty in her mirror looks and smiles.

And as a happy Lover clasps his Bride,

The fond Sea folds her round, and his brimmed
    life

Runs rippling to her inmost heart of hearts,

Until it swims a-flood with happiness;

While all the waters of her love leap back

To him exultant from a thousand hills.

From his salt virtue comes her northern sweetness.

With his bluff breezes how he doth embrace her!

How his rough kisses set her rose a-bloom!

Once in his rousëd wrath he lifted up

A mighty Armada in his arms, and dasht

It into sea-drift at his Mistress' feet.

And still he threatens with the voice of storms

The plots of all Invaders: still he keeps

Eternal watch around.

                        How proud in peace,

The wild white horses rear and foam along

And bring to her the harvests of a world!

How grand in war they bear her battle line

Like Strength half-smiling, perfect Power crowned

With careless grace, which seemeth to all eyes

The plume of Triumph nodding as it goes:

For visible victory sits on England's brow,
And shines upon her sails.

                  See where she sits
Holding at heart her noble dead, and nursing
Her living Children on the old brave virtue !
Wearing the rainy radiance of the morning,
A silver sweetness swimming thro' her tears ;
Feeling the glory rippling down from heaven
With smiles from all her wild flowers, her green
    leaves,
And nooks where old times live their shepherd ways.

We cannot count her heroes who lay down
In quiet graveyards when their work was done ;
But mound on mound they rise all over the land
To bar a Tyrant's path, and make his feet
To stumble like the blind man among tombs.
Her brave dead make our earth heroic dust :
Their spirit glitters in our England's face
And makes her shine, a Star in blackest night,
Calm at her heart, and glory round her head.
We think of all who fought, and who are now
Immortals in the heaven of her love ;
The Martyrs who have made of burning wrongs

Their fiery chariot, and gone up to God;
The saintly Sorrows that now walk in white;
Till faces bloom like Battle Banners flusht
All over with most glorious memories.
We are a chosen People; Freedom wears
Our English Rose for her peculiar crest,
Whoso dares touch it, bleeds upon the thorn.
It may be that the time will come again
For one more desperate struggle to the death.
The Devil's eye upon our England looks
With snaky sparkle still.   It may be they
Will rouse the tamed Berserkir rage, and make
The vein of wrath throb livid on her brow,
And wake the old Norse War-dog in her blood,
Until the long-breathed swimmer strips and springs
Afloat; strikes out and shows her battle-teeth;
The clash of conflict lightning thro' her veins!

Thrice hath our England swept the seas, an
      cleared
Her ocean path, the highways of the world,
And shall again if Robbers lie in wait.
Steadfast she stood when towering nations poured
In one wild wave their culminating power!

Thro' all that harvest-day of bloody death,
They charged in vain, and dasht upon the edge
Of her good sword, and fell, at Waterloo !
She kept the shamble slopes of Inkermann !
Thro' blood and fire and gloom of Indian War
Swam its Red Sea, and rode out the mad
    storm !
So shall we hold our own dear land with all
The old unvanquisht soul, and live to see
Their changing Empires shift like sand around
The Island Rock, the footstool of the Lord,
Where Freedom also lays her head, and rest
In calm or strife the best hopes of a world.

Great starry thoughts grow luminous in the dark !
The Bird of Hope goes singing overhead !
We cannot fear for England ; we can die
To do her bidding, but we cannot fear ;
We who have heard her thunder-roll of deeds
Reverberating thro' the centuries ;
By battle fire-light had the stories told ;
We who have seen how proudly she prepares
For sacrifice, how radiantly her face

Flasht when the Bugle blew its bloody sounds,
And bloody weather fluttered the old Flag :
We who have seen her with the red heaps round !
We who have known the mightiest powers dasht
   back
Broken from her impregnable sea-walls ;
We who have learned how in the darkest hour
The greatest light breaks out, and in the
   time
Of trial she reveals her noblest strength ;
We cannot fear for England ; cannot fear,
We who have felt her big heart beat in ours.

There's sap in the old Oak ! She lives to
   sow
The future forests with her acorns still.

Hail to thee, Mother of Nations ! mighty yet
To strive and suffer, and give overthrow !
For all the powers of nature fight for thee.
Spirits that sleep in glory shall awake,
Come down and drive thy Car of victory
Over thine enemies' necks.

> Long will they wait
> Who privily lurk to stab thee when the night
> Shall cover all in darkness.
>
> Dear old Land,
> Thy shining glories are no Sunset gleams,
> But clouds that kindle round some great new
> Dawn.

THE END.

VIRTUE AND CO., PRINTERS, CITY ROAD, LONDON

www.ingramcontent.com/pod-product-compliance
Lightning Source LLC
Chambersburg PA
CBHW030946110726
47900CB00004B/1150